Alt Hist Issue 2

Edited by Mark Lord

Contents

About Alt Hist

Submissions

Alt Hist is looking for submissions in the following categories:

Fiction

We have three pretty simple criteria subject to the editor's subjectivity:

1. Must be a short piece of fiction — under 10,000 words
2. It must be either historical fiction, historical fantasy or alternate history
3. It must be good (that's where the subjectivity comes in!)

Non-Fiction

Reviews and articles about historical fiction, alternate history books, genres and writers are welcome and criteria 2) and 3) above also apply.

Artwork

We would love to have your artwork to illustrate the magazine and website.

How To Submit

Visit http://althistfiction.com/submissions for details. Please note that you should expect a response to your submission within three months.

How to Get Alt Hist

Alt Hist is available in a printed format from www.amazon.com, and also as an e-book from the following retailers: Amazon, Apple, Barnes & Noble, Diesel, Sony, Kobo and Smashwords.

Copyright

Editorial

by Mark Lord

It seems so long ago but in reality it was just in the autumn of last year that the first issue of *Alt Hist* came out and here's the second. The reaction to our first issue was incredible. We are still selling copies of it and still getting messages from readers via Twitter, Facebook and our website about how much you enjoyed the issue. These personal messages are very important and validate the creation of this publication. We also gained some positive reviews, and some well-judged criticism as well.

It has been an amazing journey for me and I have learnt a lot. I'm not going to bore you with an explanation of how *Alt Hist* is put together, but it does take a lot more work than one might think. This means that for now *Alt Hist* will be quite an irregular publication, with perhaps 2 or 3 issues a year. This means we're not in a position to offer subscriptions, but I think the purchase of individual copies of the book and ebook seems to be working quite well for the moment.

One thing I would like to see in the future is more non-fiction pieces, especially good quality book reviews. So don't be shy. If you occasionally review historical fiction titles for your blog for instance then I'm happy to have your review included in *Alt Hist* as long as the writing is good enough. I will probably post it to the website as well as include it in the next issue.

So what's in Issue 2 of *Alt Hist*? Well we do have three book reviews as well as eight excellent stories, some short some long, but not massively long. They range from alternate history to historical fantasy to straight historical fiction. I toyed with the idea of splitting the issue into sections: Alternate History here, and Historical Fiction there for instance. But I'm glad I resisted the temptation to categorize and partition. I am a strong believer in not being constrained by genre walls. I think there's some great fiction here and whether it contains an alternate view of history or a bit of magic doesn't really matter. What is common to each is a setting in an historical past.

'Long Nights in Languedoc' by **Andrew Knighton** is another hilarious foray into the medieval past for *Alt Hist*. Andrew gave us 'Holy Water' for the first issue and I think he's been even more generous by sending us this fantastic romp through the Hundred Years War. It's got everything you could ask for: fighting, legendary monsters, relics, gags, chronicles, and more fighting, but most important of all told in a wonderfully comic style.

Apollo was the Roman god of the Sun, so he was a natural choice for NASA's early spaceships. But what if somehow rocket technology had been developed during the time of the Roman empire? They had a propellant available in naphtha and developed much of the basics of physics and mathematics that our modern civilisation is based upon. In 'The Apollo mission' **David X. Wiggin** presents us with the fantastical possibility that this might have been, and shows us what it might have been like for the first Roman in space as he is launched into the sky in what he hopes will not become a giant stone coffin.

The WW1 battle of Ypres provides the setting for 'Son of Flanders' by **William Knight**. Against the backdrop of the British assault on the German trenches, Gurner, a staff officer, must establish the truth behind the death of a young subaltern. Did he kill himself or was he murdered by one of his own men? William manages to convey the horror of the trenches and also tells an intriguing whodunit.

The underground cities built by the persecuted Christians in Turkey's Cappadocia are an amazing place. I was lucky to visit them several years ago when I was a student and they are truly incredible. **AshleyRose Sullivan** brings to life the period of history when Roman armies were sent to hunt down this new rebellious sect. 'In Cappadocia' is our first piece of flash fiction, and captures a moment in history in a brilliant way.

I think of 'The Orchid Hunters' by **Priya Sharma** as a sort of *Hearts of Darkness* for flowers, it has that feeling of impending doom and the 'horror' of European man facing the dark truth within his own psyche. We're transported to the late 19th century, a time when the Victorians were risking all just to find the latest orchid. Nothing's crazier than the truth. I'm glad to have Priya back for the second issue after her excellent 'The Bitterness of Apples' featured in the first issue and won some great plaudits from the reviewers.

'Death in Theatre' is the story of one of the iconic moments in American history: the assassination of Abraham Lincoln. **Jessica Wilson** puts us in the head of the assassin as we see what he hoped to achieve. We learn that even the death of a tyrant can be theatrical.

'The Scarab of Thutmose' by **Anna Sykora** is a rather hilarious story that takes us back to the time of the Pharaohs. Cross-dressing, crocodiles and scarabs abound. Prepare to smile as you read this one.

'The Watchmaker of Filigree Street' by **N. K. Pulley** is a delightful story set against the backdrop of the terrorist bombing campaign in 19th century London. It reminds us that such acts are not only a twentieth or twenty-first century phenomenon. Despite the disturbing setting the story is a wonderful read as we are introduced to a Japanese watchmaker whose abilities verge on the magical. Natasha is a new writer and I believe she sees this story as part of a series of linked pieces. I'm sure once you've read this you'll be eagerly awaiting more from her.

I would like to thank all the people who have made the first issue and I hope the second issue a success. Our authors, those who submitted stories but didn't quite make it, those who blogged and reviewed and linked to us, and most importantly to you the reader. Your passion for quality historical fiction is why *Alt Hist* exists.

Mark Lord

Editor of Alt Hist, The new magazine of Historical Fiction and Alternate History

Website: http://althistfiction.com/
Twitter: http://twitter.com/althist
Facebook: http://www.facebook.com/pages/Alt-Hist/125227137521391

Long Nights in Languedoc

by Andrew Knighton

From The Chronicles of Sir Richard de Motley – Parte VII:
In the noble Prince Edward of Woodstock, Sir Richard had finally found a lord
worthy of his fealty. And so he followed him on the Great Raid into Languedoc,
little realising the horrors hidden within that land ...

§

A screaming Frenchman charged towards Tobias, a falchion scything above his head. Tobias ducked and twisted, losing his footing on the leaf strewn slope. He slid backwards into a tree, bark scraping through the wool of his tunic, and ducked again as the French scout swiped at his neck. The blade thudded into the trunk.

As his opponent tried to free the sword, Tobias kicked him in the crotch. The man grimaced and curled in on himself, allowing Tobias to plunge a knife into his neck, the one clear inch of flesh between the man's hauberk and his helmet.

By the time Tobias had cleared the blood from his eyes, the Frenchman lay crumpled on the ground, a pale face amidst a crimson pool. Tobias prodded the body with his foot, just to be sure. Content that the man really was dead, he wiped the rest of the gore from his face, staining the other sleeve of his tunic. Then, with some straining and grunting, he pulled the sword from the tree. It was heavier than he was used to, but better than bringing a boot knife to a battle. He briefly contemplated taking the armour too, but decided he was better off being able to dodge and run than stumbling around under the weight of chainmail.

So much for keeping clear of the fight. He shouldn't have been surprised. The enemy were locals, and they'd be making the most of the land, watching and waiting to turn the English flank. Better to be back with the army than out here on his own.

Tobias made his way down the valley side, walking cautiously in case he ran into another scout. As the trees grew thinner the sounds of battle rose around him, the valley echoing with clashing steel and men's screams. French and English, the words blurred into an incomprehensible mess, its parts distinguishable only by tone. Anger, pain, command, desperation, they swirled over and around each other like waves breaking upon a beach, ceaseless and unforgiving.

The fighting had moved on since Tobias set off into the woods. The French had given ground, retreating along the line of the road. The English, pressing them the whole way, had left a brutal trail in their wake, the dead and injured of both sides lying scattered in the mud. The river ran red with the carnage.

The army's followers were already among the bodies, trying to distinguish Prince Edward's troops from the locals. Even with Frenchmen on both sides, a man's accent could decide whether he got bandages or a blade.

Tobias peered past them towards the fighting. It was clear now that the enemy had never meant to stop them here. He'd seen enough delaying actions to know the pattern. They'd find, once the fighting was over, that another contingent of frogs had tried to raid the baggage train, or burned the only bridge for forty miles.

Making the most of his valley side vantage, Tobias approached the battle lines. French levees and Welsh longbowmen were exchanging fire along the edge of the tree line, so he took cover in a stand of dense bushes with a view of the melee below.

He could pick out the royal standard on the right flank, near the river. Closer to him, Lord Royce's war-band were holding the centre, blades flashing as they smashed shields and skulls, their long tabards no longer blue. And here on the left, among the hundred knights contesting the bloodiest part of the field, was his employer.

Sir Richard de Motley stood out like a warhorse among ponies. Six and a half feet tall and built like a bull, he laid into the enemy without care for tactics, discipline or those around him. It was an assault that terrified friends and enemies alike, a laughing storm of destruction.

Tobias pulled a quill from his bag, sharpened the tip, and scrawled a few hasty notes on a scrap of parchment. Who Sir Richard fought alongside, a few metaphors to describe him in action, roughly how many he had slain, doubled for good measure. Most important for the chronicle, who he fought against. They wore deep green tabards, the knights' edged in silver. At the rear, the rallying point for another round of withdrawal, fluttered the lord's banner, a silver wolf on a green background.

Tobias scratched his head, trying to remember the heralds' lists from Aquitaine. He thought this banner was Geoffroi de Luna. De Luna was said not to stray far from home, and if these were his lands then they were further north than expected.

A triumphant cry rose above the rest. Sir Richard had hacked a path through the French lines, forcing those close by to follow or leave him surrounded. They wavered a moment and then surged forward, knights not wanting to be shamed, infantry not wanting to lose their pay-masters.

Their flank crumbling, the French went from slow withdrawal to full retreat, backing up the valley as fast as they could. The sun was setting on a long day's fight and the English stopped where they were, slumping over their shields or trudging to the river for a long needed drink.

Tobias stoppered his ink pot, rolled away the parchment, and went to join his master.

§

Weary from the combat, Sir Richard offered humble thanks to God for his deliverance, and set to finding a safe place for his followers to rest ...

§

Sir Richard stood amidst a litter of groaning bodies and severed limbs. The squire Adam, also bloody from the fight, had fetched the knight water and was now cleaning his sword.

Tobias bowed his head. 'Splendid fight, sir. Today will echo down the ages.'

'Of course!' Sir Richard bellowed, fiddling with the buckle of his vambrace. 'Adam, help me out of this.'

'I'd advise against, sir,' Tobias said. 'We'll have to move soon to make camp.'

'What?' Richard looked around at the gore-strewn ground, the valley sides perfect for ambushers. 'Oh.'

'There was a small, clear hilltop a mile back.' Adam passed Sir Richard the gleaming sword, as the trumpets signalled to move out. 'If we're quick we can grab a good spot.'

§

As pickets scampered off into the woods, the rest of the army got down to setting camp. Tents were raised, horses corralled, fires lit. Within minutes, the hilltop was thick with the smells of an army at rest, a mix of musty canvas, bad cooking and human waste.

Sir Richard had never been a big believer in tents.

'Adventure has no place for guy-ropes,' he'd once said.

So Tobias and Adam had to make do with a blanket thrown over a couple of fallen branches. They gathered firewood and stood staring at their little patch. Just looking at it made Tobias feel cold and wet.

'C'mon,' Adam said, rubbing his hands together. 'Let's go find some fun.'

'Can't you get into trouble on your own?' Tobias asked.

'Don't be such a Yorkshireman. C'mon.'

Adam led him through the bustling camp, following his unerring instinct for the seedy side. Around them were the shouts of orders, the pounding of hammers, the scrape of whetstones. Real soldiers never rested, not with the enemy in marching range. They spent their days and nights sharpening weapons and minds, always on edge. Tobias was no soldier, and happy that way.

They paused by a fire of a short, pox-scarred man cooking wild garlic stew. The army was full of such trail cooks, men who'd whip up a mediocre meal from whatever they could find and barter it to other soldiers.

The man didn't speak much English. Adam haggled with him in signs and stray syllables, getting them two dry scraps of bread heaped with brown slop.

They strolled on through camp, Adam looking for somewhere to sit. Tobias was too hungry for that. He'd not eaten since they marched at dawn, and his belly was gnawing on itself. He tucked straight into the food, scooping handfuls into his mouth, grateful just to have something hot and filling.

'My God.' He paused, gravy dribbling down his chin. 'That's wonderful.' He chewed contemplatively. 'The garlic really sets off the turnips. And there's something else in between, bringing it together. Thyme maybe?'

He looked back towards the cook, whose fire was now surrounded by weathered old soldiers.

Adam touched a finger to his lip.

'That's Cornish Pete. Don't tell everyone.'

They found space by the fire of a band of Cheshire longbowmen. Tobias lingered over his food while Adam challenged the bowmen to a game of knucklebones. The little white pieces rose and fell through the air as darkness settled in, and by the time they left the fire Adam had a heap of grimy pennies and several demands for a rematch.

As they walked back to their shelter, guided by the sound of Sir Richard's monstrous snoring, Tobias felt strangely content. He was foot-sore but full, and while he'd never been closer to death than today, his own fast thinking had seen him through. It was a grand night to be alive.

'Where'd you get those knucklebones?' he asked, idly curious. 'They look familiar.'

'Remember that church we passed on Friday?' Adam said.

Tobias nodded. Sir Richard always stopped to pray in churches, no matter how small and obscure. 'Leaking roof. Priest ran off before we arrived. Nice little reliquary with the finger-bones of saint ... Oh no. You didn't.'

'St Frogs-Legs don't need them anymore.' Adam jingled his purse. 'I do. And besides, he was a French saint. It ain't really desecration if it's a French saint.'

§

Tobias's bladder woke him at the first light of dawn. He trudged, shivering, towards the edge of camp, his cloak pulled tight around him. A few men still sat at the smoking remnants of fires, the tightly strung ones for whom battle was never followed by rest, but by tension and flashes of bloody memory. Tobias didn't envy them, up all night with the others' snoring and their own inner demons.

He pushed a short way into the dew-damp undergrowth, whistling for the sake of the sentries. He didn't want to accidentally piss on someone skulking in a bush, or be run through as a Frenchman.

As he relieved himself he took a moment to enjoy the scene. Dawn's first fingers caught the tops of the trees, making them stand out bright above the shadowy interior. Leaves just starting to brown at the edges, a few flowers filling the air with their fresh scent. He took a deep breath.

Something wasn't so fresh. The blood and bowel smell of recent, brutal death. He tied himself back up and contemplated heading back to camp. But curiosity, his own inner demon, got the better of him. Cursing himself for again being without a weapon, he crept towards the smell.

A body lay beneath a tree, ripped open by some wild beast. The man's face was frozen in shock. The creature, whatever it was, had managed to tear through chainmail and ribs in one blow, but the precision of that kill was offset by the wild abandon with which the beast had savaged his corpse, littering the undergrowth with shredded flesh and gnawed bones. Tatters of blue livery told Tobias that the soldier was from the Royce's retinue. A sentry, and clearly not a successful one.

§

Ever wary against the devil's works, Sir Richard sensed foul magics at play, and determined to thwart them.

§

There were other bodies. Two more sentries dead at their posts, and one of the camp whores, her body so joined with a customer that their guts couldn't be told apart.

The tone of the army was muted, relief at yesterday's victory swept away. Men twitched at a horse's whinny, kept their hands constantly at their sword-hilts.

'Wolves,' Sir Richard declared. He'd returned from a meeting of the army's knights and nobles, where they'd been given news designed to calm the men. 'Prince Edward is sending hunters into the forest to deal with them, while the rest of us keep moving.'

'What kind of wolves can shred chainmail?' Tobias asked.

'Big ones,' Richard replied, content with this explanation. 'Now strike the blanket, it's time to march.'

§

Late in the afternoon, as the army was looting a village, Tobias caught up with the hunters. The same Cheshire bowmen Adam had gamed with the previous night, they'd returned as empty handed from hunting as they had from gambling.

'If there's wolves in them woods, they're silent, invisible wolves,' one of them said.

'Shut your gob,' said their captain. 'Prince hears we've been spreading that around, we'll have more to worry about than wolves.'

The village was small, without much to loot, and there was no church for Sir Richard. Left idle, the knight and his squire sat on a fallen tree, watching rooftops go up in flames.

'... a proper part of war,' Sir Richard was explaining. 'Those who support a treasonous lord should be punished. It teaches others as well as them.'

'I get that,' Adam replied. 'But can't we just take the movables – food, coin, stuff like that. Burning hovels gives us nothing, and now they'll be too busy rebuilding to earn money for next time.'

'This isn't about property,' Sir Richard said, as a spearman wandered past with a pile of blankets. 'It's about the struggle between noble hosts, in all their chivalrous glory.'

Tobias joined them on the log and explained what he had heard. Sir Richard seemed indifferent, but Adam's face glowed with mischievous glee.

'Sir Richard,' he said, 'this could be your glorious opportunity. A chance for you to serve the prince and save the army.'

'Eh?'

'If there's more attacks, if the creatures aren't caught, it'll make men nervous. There's nothing worse than an invisible enemy. So volunteer to solve the problem. Camp out in the woods, wait for the wolves to come, kill them and impress the prince.'

'Ha! You're right!' Sir Richard rose and strode purposefully away.

'Are you mad?' Tobias hissed. 'You know he won't do this alone. Thanks to you we're going to be in the woods all night getting clawed by wolves.'

'Relax,' Adam replied. 'It's a couple of dumb beasts, his perfect opponents. And unlike those sentries, he'll know they're coming. All we have to do is keep him between us and danger, and this time tomorrow we'll all be heroes.

'Plus I know a man who'll pay well for wolf pelts.'

Tobias thought of the sentry's chest, torn open so quick no-one had even heard a scream. Then he thought of his chronicle and the story this might make. The tingle of fear remained, but was nothing next to the anticipation.

§

All through the night Sir Richard stood alert, a lone guardian, ready to face whatever danger might befall.

§

Tobias could hear a growl in the darkness, so soft and smooth it was almost comforting.

'They're here,' he whispered, backing away from the tree line.

Sir Richard and the squire Adam were playing knucklebones in the middle of the empty clearing.

'Ha! Three!' Richard exclaimed, white lumps balanced on the back of his scarred hand.

'Three, eh?' Adam carefully collected the bones, rattling them in his palm. 'Best score yet. Care to bet I can't beat it?'

'I said, they're here.' Tobias's sword scraped from the scabbard. He could see the underbrush rustling in the moonlight. Too much rustling for one or two wolves. Maybe the wind. Please God, the wind.

'Ha! This penny says you can't beat three.'

Rattle, rattle, rattle.

'Four. My penny.'

'Well you'll never beat five.'

A cloud passed across the moon, plunging the clearing into deeper shadow.

'Sir Richard.' Tobias tried not to raise his voice. Never show a wild beast fear, his grandfather had said. Of course, the old codger died trampled by a boar, so maybe his wasn't the best advice.

'Six.'

'You could have cheated. It's dark.'

The cloud retreated. Silver light once more filled the clearing.

Silver light and silver fur.

Tobias stood frozen by fear. The wolves were huge, not the mangy, wild-dog things you met on the moors back home, but beasts of myth prowling out of the darkness, all razor teeth and bulging muscles.

The growl was louder now, dragging across Tobias's senses like a jagged knife.

'Sir Richard!'

The knight looked up.

'At last!' He dropped the knucklebones and drew his sword, steel hissing heavy across cloth.

Adam leapt up too, sword in hand but less forward in his stance, keeping Sir Richard between him and the wolves.

'Look at them,' Tobias said, still backing away. 'They're huge.'

'All the more glory for us when we defeat them.' Sir Richard held out a hand, blocking Tobias's retreat. 'Show some spine.'

'They'll show my spine if I stick around. Most of my ribs too.'

Reluctantly, Tobias drew his sword and lined up beside his lord.

The wolves' growling rose, then stopped.

They leapt.

One of the beasts lunged straight at Tobias. He swung his sword, batting aside the first couple of attacks. Hot blood spattered his face as, beside him, Sir Richard sliced a leg from one wolf and caved in another's head. Adam was busy too, fending off two attackers with fast, unsettling lunges that did little damage but kept the wolves at arms' length.

'Where's my penny?' the squire asked.

'What penny?' Richard caught a leaping wolf by the throat and punched its nose in with his pommel.

'For that last toss of the bones.' Adam drew a flick of blood and a sharp yelp. 'I won. You pay me a penny.'

'Now?' Sir Richard asked, throwing one wolf at another.

'You can owe me ...' Adam leapt aside, narrowly evading razor sharp teeth.

'Debt is usury.' Sir Richard's sword slashed through the flank of Tobias's attacker, even as two more headed for the knight. 'Usury is a sin.' He yanked his purse from his belt and flung it to Adam. 'Now we are even.'

'At least.'

'Is this really the time?'

Another wolf leapt at Tobias. He raised his sword, point out, catching the beast in the chest. His arm shuddered as the blade sank between its ribs. Blood burst forth, but the beast's weight carried it forward, knocking him to the ground.

Tobias lay winded, sucking breath back into his lungs. As soon as he could move he rolled over, scrabbling for his sword. It was just out of reach, buried in the creature's chest.

He scrambled across the shadow-striped clearing, reaching for the weapon. But as he went to pull it free, a paw lashed towards him.

The creature, which a moment ago had lain as though dead, twitched and moaned. It tilted its head and panted like laughter. Its chest heaved with the noise, fur and flesh rippling around the wound. Raw strands of muscle writhed and there was a scraping cry of steel over bone as Tobias's sword fell from the wolf's body onto the blood-soaked grass. Tobias watched in horror as flesh filled the gap where the blade had been.

Tobias glanced frantically around. Unseen by Sir Richard, two halves of a felled wolf were seeping back together behind him, while new legs sprouted from another's stumps. The knight thought he was winning, but his foes were just resting.

The wolf facing Tobias rose to its feet, blood dribbling from fearsome jaws. Tobias's sword lay between its feet, guarded by wicked claws.

Tobias scrambled backwards across the grass, the wolf stalking after him. He yanked a knife from his belt and flung it. It glanced off the creature's snout, the shallow wound healing in an instant.

The wolf drew closer, toying with Tobias. Hot, rancid breath washing over him as it planted a paw on either side of his chest. Its leering face blotted out the moon. Desperate, Tobias scrabbled around, his fingers closing on something small and hard. He flung it at the beast.

The wolf screamed. It lurched back across the clearing and collapsed in a heap. Half its head had been torn away, leaving a steaming hole.

Tobias picked up another of the small objects, blinking at it in surprise. One of Adam's knucklebones glowed in the palm of his hand.

Another wolf was loping towards him. Tobias flung the bone. It hit the creature in the flank, bursting out of its back in a spray of blood and smoke. The beast slid to a halt and lay, lifeless, by Tobias's feet.

The other wolves had Sir Richard and Adam surrounded now, injured beasts rising to attack them from all sides. Tobias scoured the ground, finding two more bones. He flung one at a wolf behind Adam. The creature screeched and ran, blood pouring from its back.

The rest turned, saw their dead companions and Tobias waving a scrap of bone. As one, they turned and fled.

Tobias looked at the body at his feet. The flesh was writhing once more, limbs twisting, fur retracting, as it turned from a wolf into a man.

§

Having thwarted the foul beasts, Sir Richard knelt in supplication before his grateful lord, bearing the bodies of the monsters he had slain.

§

The prince's physician was a French Jew, a precise man with neatly trimmed nails and beard. He took his time examining the bodies, peeling back skin and muscle one layer at a time. The tent's other occupants, all senior nobles except Sir Richard and his retainers, watched in curious silence. This was a new way to see a body taken apart, revealing details they would have missed in a fight. But despite the novelty, they were growing bored, fiddling with their armour or picking their noses.

'What can you tell us, Solomon?' Prince Edward had good royal instincts, knowing not to let armed men become restless.

The physician set down the scalpel and wiped his hands on his apron.

'He was about thirty years old,' he said. 'Noble born, second son I believe, he was well fed and sheltered. Used to joust, fenced a little, but not much of a rider. Widely read, but not what you'd call intelligent.'

'You can tell all that from a body?' Tobias blurted out in amazement, forgetting his place.

Solomon's mouth hitched up in a small smile.

'No, even my gift has its limits. I know his face from working in these parts. This is Jacques, son of the lord de Luna.'

'So what can you tell from the body?' The prince leaned forward in his chair, fingers playing with his dark beard. Here he was, twenty-five years old and the master of European chivalry, staring at a dead body. Not how Tobias had dreamed of meeting him.

'There is no anatomical sign of the transformation Sir Richard described.' Solomon pulled back one of the flaps of skin, holding a candle close to illuminate the exposed layers. 'Fur, teeth, claws, they have not merely retracted into the body, they have entirely disappeared. The bones and muscles are those of a normal man. I would be tempted to disbelieve the entire incident, if it weren't for this.'

He pointed to the wound in Jacques de Luna's chest, a burnt hole in the centre of a bruise-darkened ring.

'It is as if he were struck with inhuman strength by a red-hot poker, which then became a force akin to a cannon burst, its strength spent in only one direction, blasting his innards out of his back and cauterising what remains. I know no creature or device which could achieve this, and yet it was apparently done with a fragment of ordinary bone.'

Tobias glanced sidelong at Adam, who was innocently watching the nobles around him. Did the squire share his suspicion that the bone's effect came from its saintly origin, an awkward point they'd kept quiet about? Or was his mind elsewhere, working out who had the richest servants to fleece?

'In short,' the physician continued, 'these are unnatural creatures of considerable power. Enemies we can harm in only one way, a way that is grisly and of uncertain efficacy.'

Now it was his turn for the sidelong glance, eyeing Tobias, and by implication his story, with suspicion.

There was an expectant silence. The nobles, unsure what to think, waited to follow their prince's lead.

'We can't go back the way we came,' the prince said at last. 'Too many enemies, not enough food. But we're not here to fight devils either. So we press on. Move quickly and get out fast, back to where we can punish frog John's followers with ease. That means little rest and no pillage until we're out of Luna's lands.

'Be ready to march at dawn. And while they're waiting, tell your men to equip themselves with bone. Perhaps we can all find the strength of a cannon blast.'

§

The moon was rising into a soft grey dusk as they marched through another nameless village. It was a place that clearly mattered locally, containing a ramshackle watermill and a lichen-stained church with neatly ranked graves. But to the prince's army, it wasn't even a stop on the road. For two days now they'd used every moment of daylight, and there'd be no stopping until full darkness hid the road from their feet.

Sir Richard, Adam and Tobias marched near the head of the column. Their encounter with the wolf-men had given them a certain prestige, saving them from their old place at the dust-choked rear of the army. With prestige came an expectation – that, if need be, they could defeat the creatures again.

Outside the village was an open meadow, beyond which their route was again flanked by trees, long shadows darkening the road. As they drew near, Tobias caught a glimpse of movement in the tree line. He nudged Adam.

'Look, over there.'

'What?'

'Something moved.'

'Of course something moved. It's a forest. Its full of moving things. Deer, boar, squirrels, even trees blowing in the wind.'

'There is no wind. And it wasn't an animal sort of movement.'

'Then what sort was it?'

'I don't know. Just ... not those.'

'Getting jumpy?'

'You should be too. We're ...'

Thud.

Thud, thud, thud.

Thud.

Around them, men fell screaming, crossbow bolts protruding from bodies, arms, shields. Tobias looked around for cover, but there was none. They were in an open field, surrounded on three sides by woodlands. The perfect place to deliver an ambush, and the worst to receive it.

'Ha!' Sir Richard exclaimed. 'At last!'

And with that he was off, rushing towards the tree line, shield held out in front, chainmail jangling as he ran. Others followed, whether mistaking him for a commander or just eager to see action. Even Tobias joined the charge, rather than stand still and be shot.

As they raced forwards there came a second surprise. From the forest to their left rose a great howl, and a force of armed men burst from the trees, charging the English flank. But these were no ordinary men. They were huge brutes, armed and armoured but clawed and snarling, their long faces furred, clawed feet carrying them fast across the meadow. Half-man half-wolf, each one was a vision of destruction.

The Cheshire archers were on the left flank. They loosed a volley straight into the attackers, piercing armour and shields to no effect. The beasts kept coming.

As the archers pulled back, other men stepped forward with chunks of bone, wary expressions on their faces. As the creatures drew near they flung the white lumps. One hit the foremost wolfman and he cried out. But it was a cry of laughter, not pain, and the throwers barely had time to draw their swords before the beasts were among them. They hacked with swords and claws, leapt and gouged, snapped at men's heads with their jagged teeth. Tobias saw one take a dagger through the throat and fall to the ground, only to draw the blade out and turn it on its owner.

Where minutes before the flower of English soldiery had marched towards victory, instead there was panic, slaughter, and retreat.

Sir Richard was in the thick of the action, hacking to left and right. Each creature he hit rose to its feet again, but he was oblivious, caught up in the thrill of action. They could come at him again and again, he'd have a new move every time, and a grin with it.

But one man's ferocity wasn't enough. They needed something more, and fast.

'Come on.' Tobias grabbed Adam's arm, dragging him back towards the village. 'I've got an idea.'

'Is it to run like hell?' Adam asked. 'Because right now, I could do that.'

Back here, the English troops were busy too. Though only facing ordinary soldiers, and not the crazed beasts at the front, they were still surrounded on three sides, unprepared, and fighting on unfamiliar ground. They were retreating slowly, but they were retreating.

Tobias reached the church and tried the door. It was solidly built and bolted from inside. Nothing short of a battering ram was getting through it.

He bit back a curse. He didn't want to compound his impending sins by blaspheming on holy ground.

'There must be another way in,' he said, glancing up at the leaded windows. Was it sacrilege to break church glass? Could he even climb that far up the walls?

'You'd be amazed at how often one of these windows gets broken in a storm,' Adam said. 'Let me go look.'

Tobias lurked in the porch shadows, watching out for wolves or soldiers and trying not to hear a tinkle of broken glass.

There was an angry shout, swiftly cut short, then a thunk of sliding bolts. The door swung open on Adam's grin.

'Dreadful state, this place,' he said. 'They've left a priest cluttering up the nave.'

Tobias stepped inside, glancing guiltily at the cross above the altar. It was a cheap affair, local wood carved by local hands, one side warping with age. The whole place was lit with cheap candles that sputtered and dribbled onto the granite flagstones. Still, it was God's house.

He knitted his hands and sank to one knee, trying not to look at the robed body beneath the pulpit.

'Lord, please forgive a pair of humble sinners, but we need this more than you. Amen.'

'What now?' Adam was levering open the collection box with a knife.

'Grab anything holy. Crosses, incense burners, communion plates. But remember, we're only borrowing it.'

'Borrowing, huh.' Adam started scooping up pewter jugs and bowls, anything marked with a crucifix. 'I get it. How about that?'

He pointed at the big wooden cross.

'Too unwieldy.' Tobias was filling jugs with holy water from the font.

'If we break it up we can get a lot of holy weapons. They'll be pointy, too.'

Tobias stood, unable to believe his ears. It was an appalling idea, blasphemous, unthinkable, ingenious.

He couldn't bring himself to do it.

'I'm going now,' he said. 'Bring whatever you can, but don't take too long – we don't have much time.'

He hurried out the door, the creak of splintering wood swiftly replaced by the roar and crash of battle.

The village was lit by the flickering of a hundred torches, held aloft by the rear ranks of the French force. Their flanks weren't attacking any more, just channelling the English, keeping them in a confined space for the wolfmen to attack. There were more French behind the village, blocking off any line of retreat.

Fear was spreading through the English troops. Word of the carnage at the front had run back through the line. The tension that had festered since the deaths of the sentries, stewed up over two tiring days, twisted into knots of panic. Small groups made dashes for the tree line, only to be cut down by crossbow bolts. Lords tried to control their men, but it was hard to assert any order in the darkness between huts and pigsties. Even the prince himself, stood beneath his banner by the village well, was barely able to keep the army from fleeing into the deadly night.

The panic was like a contagion, a jittering, whispering gesture that spread from man to man, growing as it went. Tobias could feel it infecting him, an urge to turn and run, to hide, to do anything but face the horror ahead.

He pressed it down and pushed through to the front line. Here the bravest and most desperate were holding up the monstrous attack. They knew by now that they couldn't harm their foes, but they tried to keep them at swords' length. It was a sad, brutal spectacle, these blood-spattered warriors, drenched with sweat, stooping under the weight of armour and exhaustion as, one by one, they fell to the oncoming horde.

And at the heart of it all, roaring and bellowing and fighting worth a dozen men, was Sir Richard.

Tobias hesitated for a moment. Once he got close there'd be no coming back. The creatures would have him.

But if this didn't work they'd all be dead within an hour. What choice did he have?

A beast, fully wolf, was scrambling up Sir Richard's shield and over his head, trying to bury its claws in his back. Tobias gave one last, urgent prayer, gripped a jug and lunged.

The wolf blinked in surprise as water splashed its fur, then screamed and fell, its face melting like fat over an open fire.

Sir Richard turned and another wolf leapt at his back. Tobias flung the contents of a second jug, splashing the knight and sending the beast back in holy agony.

'Dip your sword in this.' Tobias held out a bowl.

'Eh?'

'A priest told me.' Well, he might have if he'd been conscious.

Sir Richard dipped his sword in the holy water and turned to face the fray. Another beast was rushing at him, this one still half man. He parried one blow of its axe, caught another on his shield, and brought his sword up through a gap in its defences. The blade cut through its arm like a knife through water, leaving the creature staring in shock at a smoking stump. Another swing of the knight's sword sent its head flying.

The other wolves sensed something amiss and began to back off. But they'd barely had a moment to regroup when the air filled with hissing and two dozen arrows wobbled over the knights' heads, landing in the wolves' midst. They howled and screamed as a second volley fell among them, slaying some and leaving others writhing in agony.

Tobias turned to see the Cheshire longbowmen draw their strings a third time, long wooden splinters tied to the tips of their arrows. Adam stood among them, grinning and waving a candlestick.

By now other knights had followed Sir Richard's lead and dipped their blades in Tobias's jug. As the enemy infantry stood uncertainly at the edge of the clearing, watching their masters writhe and scream, Sir Richard raised his sword.

'For Edward and England!' he yelled.

As one, the English force charged.

§

The holy spirit flowed through Sir Richard, guiding his blows, until not a single beast remained. The village was saved from the abominations, and the army free to march on.

§

Dawn found Tobias with a band of soldiers, flinging bodies onto a fire.

'Were these all monsters?' Adam asked.

'Just the knights, I think,' Tobias said, 'but I'm not taking any chances.'

He picked up a handful of severed fingers and flung them into the flames.

'Ha! No abomination can stand before God and a good blade!' Sir Richard said.

'Indeed.' Tobias turned to watch as the English troops, now free to take their time, set about looting the village.

Price Edward was approaching, followed by the usual entourage of nobles and servants.

'Good work, Sir Richard,' the prince said. 'My congratulations to you and your men. But tell me, how did you know that holy water on the swords and arrows would work?'

'We're English,' Sir Richard declared with every sign of sincerity. 'Of course God would be on our side.'

Andrew spent six years studying history, and with the advent of *Alt Hist* he's finally putting that learning to good use. 'Long Nights in Languedoc' was partly inspired by his dissertation on warfare in the era of the Black Prince, a time when chivalry meant telling people you were planning to massacre them. You can read another of Sir Richard and his companions' adventures, 'Leprosaria', in the *Roll the Bones* anthology, out now from Fight On! Publications. He's had over thirty short stories published in magazines and websites. Find out more at andrewknighton.wordpress.com.

The Apollo Mission

by David X. Wiggin

The legionnaire awoke, surprised to see that he was still alive. He had dreamt of fire and pain and an endless fall that filled the blue void with screams. Pink light from the rising sun oozed over the darkness of the hut around the edges of the window shades. A knock came at the door. It was time.

He dressed slowly, keeping his mind focused on each individual task. He meticulously double-checked every strap of his armour and carefully avoided the thoughts that made his heart beat like a sparrow's. A smartly dressed regiment of Rome's finest awaited him outside. They saluted him in the manner befitting a patriot and he returned their salute in the manner of a man too proud to show his terror. They lead him—silent but for the clank of their weapons and the beat of their sandals upon the dust—and he let himself be led like a docile ox to the slaughter. He looked up at the dawning sky as they marched and saw puffs of cloud aimlessly hanging above like Jupiter's lost sheep. Soon he would be high above them, looking down at their backs with an eagle's disdain. Would they look so soft and gentle then? None but the gods and Icarus had ever beheld such a view until now.

Beyond the clouds shone Venus. He beetled his brow in a squint, trying to pierce the veil of distance between them. Would she be so beautiful when she was close by, and would he be damned—like poor Actaeon—for such sights? These questions weighed upon him like great stones, but he knew that they mattered not at all. He was a dutiful Roman soldier, chosen for this honour because of his courage and his strength. He would do as they asked and no less. To act otherwise would mean dishonour, worse than death. His questions would be answered inevitably anyway, regardless of his doubts.

The sun hadn't cleared the horizon when they reached the camp. The smell of sulphur and offal and other stinks that could not be named clogged their nostrils. They had all been ill the first day but by now they were used to the stench in the manner of a hog to its own reek. The legionnaire studied the rounded arrow-shaped obelisk at the centre of the camp for the thousandth time. Its size was such that he could make out the details—painted prayers to the gods, frescos of griffins, pegasi, and flying chariots—along its shaft. He had smiled the first time he had seen it and joked:

'This is to be my coffin?'

Now he set his jaw tight. *This is to be my coffin.*

As they entered the camp, horns blared. Workers and soldiers stopped to watch the procession pass. Some yelled encouragement; others jested, but most were silent. There were no words yet for what they were about to witness.

The Apollo Mission

Dignitaries awaited them at the base of the obelisk: generals, priests, and scholars. Great men all. They told him he was doing a great service for the empire. Poets would sing his name for centuries. A year before, his heart would have blazed with the kindling of such praise, but now he scarcely heard it. Against the infinite above, these men were nothing. All his attention was on the pointing finger of the obelisk. At its base, men were packing a thick black paste whose incineration would provide the force to propel the tower over the peak of Olympus and into the great sky like an arrow shot into the heart of the sea. He would drown in that void, he would vanish into it and nothing of him would remain. These men who were sweetening his annihilation with candied words were terrified as well. Even they could not grasp the enormity of what they were attempting.

Finished with flattery, the priests performed their blessing ceremony before he was lead through the threshold of the sky ship. It was dark within-- what little air there was stank of the explosive mixture. Sure-handed slaves tightened the straps that held him fast to his chair. A single window was provided for him, small, round, at the level of his eyes. Through that window he could see the sun rising. The golden disk flashed as it broke free from the earth, causing the legionnaire to screw up his eyes and look away. The slaves finished their work and quickly departed, muttering in their strange tongues. They sealed the entrance with bricks and mortar. Not so much as a crack remained. There was only darkness, the light from a single window the size of a child's fist, the reek of the phlogistian compound mixed with fear, and the legionnaire.

He could smell the smoke from their torches. A chant rose up, a paean to Jupiter, to Mercury, and to Apollo—whose name this mad journey was in. The legionnaire felt light-headed and slightly mad, as though he were drunk. A small smile twisted its way onto his face and he fought the urge to laugh for fear of embracing the terror that prowled the borders of his sanity. The earth below him was about to explode with the violence of angry Etna—Typhon raging in the heart of her depths. He had seen the tests done with pigs, horses, apes, and slaves. A third had died screaming in flames, another third had vanished in spectacular explosions, and the final third had made it into the air only to career about the sky before smashing nose-first into the ground miles away. None had survived. In all his years of service, of all the ways he'd pictured his death, he had never imagined anything approaching this.

His last thoughts, before the sound of thunder drowned them out were, for the first time in weeks, of his wife and daughter back in Rome. Then a force struck his front with the weight of a slain man and he felt a sudden eruption against his back, as though a thousand hands had shoved him as one, and his stomach and throat were filled with a sickening sense of freedom, as though he was plummeting- but he knew he was not falling at all, quite the contrary. His window was obscured by black smoke and the glow of flame but it soon cleared and he saw a blurred mass of blue and white and green and brown racing by outside. The chair he was strapped to shook and rattled until he became convinced that his teeth would fall out, yet some divine power kept the stone cylinder intact. Somehow he had sat atop an explosion whose kiss was powerful enough to hurl ten tons of weight into the sky and had survived. He did not know what frightened him more: the fact that he could have died horribly, or that he was still alive and hurtling hundreds of feet deeper with every passing second into the bluest depths of the sky.

Gradually, the obelisk began to slow its ascent as the violence of the initial explosion was stretched thin by time and distance. There came the sound of cracking wood, of cloth holding taut against rebellious winds and the legionnaire knew that the many hidden sails intended to serve as wings had successfully opened along the ships length. They travelled smoothly now, gently riding the currents of the upper regions. His vision steady—though his body still shook from terror and the sudden, incredible cold—the legionnaire looked out his small window to watch the world with Jupiter's eyes.

The land below was too far away to be seen. It had become a mass of blue-blackness, a great silent sea. He was above men, above mountains, above the birds, the clouds, the gods, the very dome of the sky. The emptiness shocked him more than the force of the explosion had.

The prayers of the priests, the superstitions of his mother, the poems of Homer and Virgil: these were lies he realized. There were no gods here in this void. No stern keepers of nature and man. Only silence and blue. Strangely, this understanding did not frighten him. What need had man for divinities when he could fly so high? This was a new sea, incalculably vast. Who could imagine the beasts that dwelt so high in the air, the treasures that might be mined from the vacuum by clever men? He envisioned fortresses hovering above the world like small moons. Clouds whipped into roads that ran in every conceivable direction. He saw an empire that never ended, but grew eternally. A sense of peace came over him for the first time in his life. The Roman civilization was not withering into decadence as so many cynics whispered these days. The true Empire, with its destiny so clearly intended for the stars, had not even begun.

For that moment of revelation—though it was likely no longer than a second, perhaps two—the stone arrow hung in the void, unmoving in defiance of nature and then, slowly at first, but with gathering speed, it began to fall.

David X. Wiggin spent his childhood wandering the globe and attending schools in places as diverse Japan and Singapore, Russia and Virginia. These days he leads a more settled life in Brooklyn with his wife and two cats; working odd jobs, keeping the house tidy, and generally doing what he pleases. He has previously published stories with *Alienskin* and *Steampunk Magazine* and is currently working on a novel set in 1920's Tokyo.

Son of Flanders

by William Knight

A Very Light arced through the air, illuminating the sodden communication trench in a pale, spectral glow.

Gurner froze in the glare and waited with bated breath for the light to fizzle out, his wide eyes plastered to the starless sky.

'Best be moving along, Captain,' his guide said, barely disguising the annoyance in his voice. He was an old hand, out since 1914, and had little patience for the New Army officers flooding the ranks.

'Right, lead on Corporal.'

They slunk off through the darkness of the trench. It was less a trench than a pit filled with mud and laid with slimy duckboards.

The guide slipped and fell into the mud, cursing.

'Bloody mud,' he hissed. 'Watch your step, sir, pit 'ere.'

Gurner carefully picked his way over the shell-hole. He was glad the guide was leading the way. In many places the duckboards had been removed or blown away, revealing gaping pits filled with sludge, sometimes waist deep.

They reached a traverse and the guide paused, muttering to himself. Somewhere a machine-gun clattered away, a German Maxim by the sound of it. A moment later a British Lewis gun answered. The sounds of exploding shells grew louder as they neared the front, the ground vibrating under the assault. More Very Lights stormed the occluded sky, bleeding their false daylight.

Gurner felt the familiar tightening in his stomach, the cold creep of fear up his spine. He had to resist the urge to turn around and bolt down the trench. The guide seemed little worried, though. He continued to slog through the mud, cursing and muttering in his thick cockney accent. Gurner could understand the man's anger. Rather than retiring to the rest billets with the rest of his company in Poperinghe, he was detailed to lead a brigade officer up through the mud to the firing-line. Hardly a choice assignment.

To make matters worse the trench system was in shambles. The marshy fields of Flanders were soggy under the best of conditions and with the summer of 1917 being one of the wettest in recent history, it had turned the Belgian lowlands into a bog.

They stumbled into a fire-bay. Several troops sat on the fire-step, sullen looking and drenched with rain. One was singing a popular tune under his breath.

'*There's a long, long trail a-winding,*

Into the land of my dreams,'

'Oi, mate, where the Lanc's at?' his guide asked.

One of the Tommy's shifted, scratching at the chats. He was covered from head to toe in mud, and had a soggy Woodbine hanging from his lips.

'Down that way,' he said dispiritedly, waving a lazy arm.

They continued slogging through the mud until they reached a stretch of caved in trench. A machine-gun spat, almost right on top of them, and Gurner hunched instinctually. They'd reached the front line.

Gurner carefully poked his head over the trench and stared into no man's land. It was dark, but he could make out some of the features of the landscape. Broken stumps of trees curled out of the ground like claws and he could make out the burnt out carcass of a tank.

In the distance he could see the flash of artillery on Pilckem ridge, high above the battlefield below.

A rat scurried across the parapet; a huge black monstrosity the size of a small dog, glutted on the dead of the battlefield.

'Fool's errand,' he muttered to himself. Already the heavy clay was caked to his uniform and his helmet felt twice as heavy, the lining digging into his forehead. Water already sluiced over the top of his gum boots and his puttees were soaked through. He was thoroughly miserable by the time they'd reached their destination.

A tall officer of the Lancashire Fusiliers, who introduced himself as Oldham led him the rest of the way; his guide slinking off into the gloom without so much as a fare-thee-well.

They waded through the thigh deep mud till they reached the entrance to a dugout, built beneath the parados. It was facing the wrong way, towards the enemy lines, as the trench had recently been taken from the Germans.

Two guards stood on either side of the entrance with dour expressions on their soot covered faces, and stared daggers at Gurner's red gorget tabs. Their Lee Enfield rifles were clabbered with mud, and hardly looked fit for the firing-line.

Oldham pulled back the heavy gas blanket and led Gurner down the slippery wooden slats into the dugout. A sergeant-major followed them down. Gurner had to watch his steps carefully as a thin stream cascaded down the steps, making them slick and hazardous.

The dugout was deep and wide and fortified with timber. In the corner a coal brazier burned, illuminating the space with pale, flickering light. Soiled water leeched from the ceiling in drips.

There was a cot in the corner of the dugout, resting atop some empty crates. Gurner moved slowly to the corner as a shell rattled above, making the brazier flicker and casting long shadows over the occupant of the cot.

A young officer lay dead on the mottled cot in full khaki, a bullet hole through his temple. A Webley revolver lay on the ground beside his outstretched hand.

Gurner knelt in front of the cot and examined the body of Subaltern W.H. Levy, formerly of the Royal Warwickshire Regiment.

He was young, no more than a lad. Eighteen or nineteen, if Gurner had to guess. His uniform was stained with Flanders mud and Gurner could tell from the smell, or lack thereof, that he'd only been dead a few hours.

'Is his batman still present?' Gurner asked.

'Yes, sir,' Oldham responded.

'Have him sent down, please, Lieutenant.'

'Right away, sir.' He mumbled a quick order to the sergeant-major who disappeared back up the mouldering steps.

'Forgive me for asking, sir, but why is brigade taking such an interest?' Oldham asked. 'One officer gone west is hardly a matter for an investigation, when we got the Boche not two-hundred yards away.'

Gurner shrugged his shoulders as the officer voiced the very same concerns he'd delivered to the brigadier himself, not three hours ago. It seemed strange to be investigating the death of one man in the middle of a battle that was claiming so many lives.

'Well, Oldham. This lad here happens to be the son of a financial counsellor to Winston Churchill, the Minister of Munitions. A high-ranking and powerful counsellor if I understood the brigadier correctly. And he doesn't want to send the man a telegram saying his son committed suicide at the front.'

'I see,' Oldham said. 'Why'd they send you?'

Why indeed?

'I was a police constable in Wellesbourne, before the war.'

Gurner rubbed his chin. He'd been a constable for only two years when the war had started, and mostly his duties had to do with corralling the local drunkards or solving domestic disputes. He'd never even seen a dead body before joining the army, let alone investigated a potential homicide, and had told the brigadier as much, but the old man had sent him anyway.

He picked the Webley up off the ground and opened the cylinder. It held five cartridges; one chamber was empty. A spent shell lay lodged in the mud.

He was about to write the young subaltern's death off as a suicide, when he noticed something curious. The man had a welt under his left eye, a purplish bruise that puffed out the skin and sat stark against his pallid skin.

'That's curious,' he mumbled aloud.

He stood up and looked around the dugout. Over in the corner next to the brazier sat a rough-hewn table and chair. He walked over. The table was bare but for a sheet of dirty paper and a smudge of a taper, burnt down to ruin.

Gurner picked up the letter. It had been written by Levy. The paper was smudged and muddied but he could make out the writing. The penmanship was poor, the writing scratched and shaky as if written with a tremulous hand.

'Dear Louise,

I hope this letter finds you well. I received your last package and thank you for the sweets and the pomade to counteract the effects of the lice. However, the little buggers seem to thrive on the stuff. I cannot tell you more, than that I am in the Ypres salient at last. It is as bad as they say. The mud is terrible and clings to everything and the shelling never ceases. I went over-the-top yesterday to lead a patrol and met with some difficulty, for which I hope God will see fit to forgive me one day, as I cannot seem to forgive myself. I ...'

It was there the letter ended. Gurner took off his helmet, set it down on the table and sat down in the rickety chair. His curiosity was piqued. While the tone of the letter certainly wasn't cheerful, it wasn't what you'd expect a man to write before he shot himself in the head. And why wouldn't he have finished the letter? It didn't make any sense. And what was the difficulty he'd mentioned? Gurner frowned and folded the letter, stuffing it into a pocket of his grimy tunic. Perhaps the brigadier had been right about there being something amiss.

'Captain,' Oldham said. 'Is it true we're to take Pilckem Ridge?'

Gurner sighed. He turned around and studied the officer. He was tall with a thin, sallow face and high patrician cheekbones, his eyes were rimmed with purple rings that denoted many a sleepless night.

'Is this your first time out, Lieutenant?' he asked.

Oldham nodded, his lips forming into a tight smile. He could tell the lad was windy, but he was maintaining his composure to the best of his ability. He reminded Gurner of himself when he'd first been sent out to the trenches--a young officer straight from the three-month officer training camp and thrust into the blood bath on the Somme. Most of his unit had perished in Gommecourt and he'd afterwards been transferred to brigade as an Intelligence Officer.

The memory of the carnage on the Somme still brought him horrible nightmares.

'Pilckem Ridge is the target, son, and that smudge of brick dust that used to be Langemarck.'

Oldham groaned. 'When do we attack?'

'As soon as the rain lets up, my boy, as soon as the rain lets up.' Not that it would do the attacking troops much good. Langemarck was on high ground and the Germans had fortified the position with pillboxes, made with four-foot thick concrete walls and studded with Maxims. Not to mention that no-man's-land was a swamp and near impassable.

The sergeant-major trudged back down the stairs, leading along a scared young boy with a shock of red hair poking out from under his dented helmet, and a pimpled face. The boy was shaking visibly, and when he saw Lieutenant Levy's body in the corner he started to whimper; strangled sobs escaping from between his thin lips. From the boy's frail appearance, Gurner pegged him for a conscript.

'All right, son, all right,' the sergeant-major said, patting the boy on the back. He turned to Gurner. 'It's perishin' jerry what's got him all upset, sir.'

Gurner could tell the boy was close to cracking.

'You were Lieutenant Levy's batman, son?' he asked.

'Aye, s-s-sir,' he answered. 'As it w-were.' His eyes darted nervously to the corpse than back to Gurner.

'Can you tell me anything about his frame of mind, over the past few days?'

The boy looked confused. 'Can't rightly say, sir. I just got here myself a couple days ago. Can't figure why he'd go and off himself.'

'Who was his batman before you, then?'

The whole dugout shivered as a shell hit above, and the timber supports started moaning ominously. The boy let out a cry of alarm.

'Speak up, lad. Who was his batman?' He meant to keep his tone civil, but to be honest he had the wind up, and he didn't want to spend one second longer in the front line then he had to.

'I-I don't know, sir.'

Well, that just about figured in Gurner's mind. He stood up and put his helmet back on. It was time to go and have a chat with the brigadier. That was *if* he managed to get through the shell-fire without getting hit, as it sounded like the Germans were laying down a heavy barrage; though he wouldn't have minded a nice blighty one at this point.

§

Brigadier Rolfe had set up his headquarters in the ruins of the Chateau de Mymes in Poperinghe. What was once an imposing mansion in the Flemish style had been reduced to a shelled-out wreck. Crumbling masonry dotted the front walkway and the shingled roof was shattered and pitted with holes. The render had peeled and flaked away on the façade leaving the stone walls barren and covered with sickly grey lichen.

After a delay of an hour, Gurner was led into the brigadier's office. It had once been an elegant two-floor library with a spiral staircase, but most of the books had been spirited away, and it now smelled of damp and gunpowder. A large-caliber shell had torn a jagged, gaping hole out of the far wall. The hole had been covered with a canvas tarp, which rippled and shrieked as it met the battering winds.

He waited patiently while the brigadier finished arranging papers on his desk in an imperious fashion. The man had a rotund face and a bristling white moustache, and was a relic of the old, professional army. He looked down on the duration soldiers of the New Army who'd flooded the recruiting stations in the aftermath of Lord Kitchener's call for soldiers.

The brigadier slumped back in his chair and slowly poured himself a glass of whiskey. He drained it in one gulp, and then looked up at Gurner as if noticing him for the first time.

'What did you find out, Captain?'

Gurner cleared his throat. 'Sir, I examined the body of Subaltern Levy, and while there were some unexplained discrepancies, it appears the lad committed suicide.'

The brigadier furrowed his bushy brow. 'What discrepancies?'

Gurner explained about the bruise under the subaltern's eye and produced the letter, sliding it across the dull surface of the desk. The brigadier glanced down at the letter and then poured himself another glass of whiskey, not bothering to read it.

'Well, it looks like you have some further investigating to do; I won't keep you from it.' The brigadier went back to shuffling his papers. 'Dismissed.'

Gurner started to say something but thought better of it. He snapped a smart salute, which the brigadier ignored, and left the chateau quickly.

The clouds were thick in the sky, grey with the portent of rain...always the rain.

A group of squalid children descended on him as he walked down the rubble-strewn street.

'Bully beef, Tomm-ee? Biscuits? Pleeease?' they begged in shrill tones.

When he tried to explain that he didn't have any food, their plaintive squawks increased in volume and tempo. He grumbled and lowered his head, trying to ignore them as they jostled and scrambled about him, holding out their dirty little hands.

A shell landed a block over with a mighty roar, throwing up a plume of acrid dust, it was followed a second later with the sound of toppling masonry. The children scattered into the wind and Gurner walked the rest of the way alone.

§

The sky was dull and a beastly cold rain had started to fall by the time Gurner found the location of the Seventh Royal Warwicks. They were bivouacked about three miles north of Poperinghe in De Wippe Camp, a tattered arrangement of ramshackle huts and mud-stained tents. It had been a thoroughly miserable journey as the roads had all been zeroed in by the German artillery, so he'd had to constantly throw himself down onto the muddy ground or hide in shell holes filled with tepid brown water at the side of the road.

Gurner gritted his teeth and slogged along, wrapping his sodden greatcoat tight around his shoulders. Not for the first time, he bitterly challenged the intelligence of Field Marshall Douglas Haig for launching yet another operation in the Ypres salient; a place of limited strategic importance and inaccessible heights held by the enemy.

After several fruitless queries, he was finally directed to the officer's hut, a long, narrow confusion of mouldy boards, with rabbit wire beds and a lonely coal-stove in the corner belching black smoke. A table had been set up near the stove and a group of officers were gathered around it.

Gurner walked over to them. They were playing Pontoon and a pile of grubby francs sat in the centre of the table.

'I'm looking for Captain Greenfoss,' he said.

A young man with dark features, wearing the ribbon of the Military Cross glanced at him, narrowing his eyes when he saw Gurner's red tabs. 'I'm Greenfoss,' he said in a suspicious tone.

'I need to speak with you in private.'

Greenfoss smirked and glanced at his fellow officers, who were also smirking. 'What about?'

Gurner leaned over him. 'Subaltern Levy.'

Greenfoss looked stricken and stood up stiffly. They walked over to one of the cots and he sat down, with Gurner taking the cot across from him.

'What do you want to know?'

'You were Levy's superior officer, I was hoping you might have some insight into his death.'

Greenfoss scrunched his face in confusion. 'I'm not sure I follow you. Far as I know, Levy killed himself.' The Captain lit up a crooked cigarette and blew out the smoke, glancing nervously over his shoulder. Gurner had the feeling the man was hiding something.

'Well, Captain, that's what I'm here to find out.'

Greenfoss took a nervous puff on his Woodbine, and Gurner noticed his hands were shaking. He took the letter out of his breast pocket and handed it to Greenfoss. The captain took it, scanned it quickly then offered it back. Gurner ignored him.

'Could you tell me the incident Levy was speaking of, Captain Greenfoss?'

'I'm sure I have no idea. Look...' he leaned forward. 'Can I speak plainly with you?'

Gurner nodded. 'I wish you would.'

Greenfoss squinted. 'Levy was a windy lad. The boy had nerves you wouldn't believe. A shell could land a hundred yards away and he'd start shaking like a Larch in high wind. Tried to talk to him, I told him--you just got to chance it lad, if a shell's bound for you, it's going to get you and no stopping it. I talked to the colonel about getting him transferred behind the lines, told him the boy was too timorous for the firing line, but he was the son of some blasted minister or such, and the colonel wouldn't hear of it. So I was stuck with a blasted coward who'd of been better use in the cook line, than leading men into battle.'

Gurner listened calmly while the captain spoke. The man still had a nervous shake, which made him curious.

'So you think he killed himself, then?'

Greenfoss nodded. 'Aye. It's a horrible thing, horrible. But it does happen from time to time. Some of the boys just can't muck it. His first time in the lines and he's sent to Ypres. It doesn't get much worse than that.'

Gurner had to agree with him there.

'Do you recall the name of his batman?' he asked. 'Before the current one, that is?'

Greenfoss lowered his gaze. 'Yes, it was Turner; a friendly lad, well liked in the regiment.'

'What happened to him?'

'Killed while on patrol with Levy.'

Gurner could tell there was something more to the story, but decided not to press him.

'Can you direct me to Levy's old section? I'd like to speak to them.'

Greenfoss nodded and agreed eagerly, all too happy to help Gurner get on his way. He handed the letter back to Gurner and then wiped his hand on his tunic as it were soiled.

§

The men of Levy's section were sitting round a small scrub of fire, 'chatting' their uniforms, a common pastime for the Tommy. Gurner himself had done it on more than one occasion. The lice thrived in the deep woolen seams of the khaki and could only be dislodged by running a flame across the seam. It was an unappealing but necessary task if one wanted to maintain one's sanity.

The men joked and laughed against the steady thrum of the shells, which lit up the Eastern horizon. It was the opening barrage for the upcoming attack on Pilckem Ridge and the smudge of mortar dust and splinters which was all that remained of the town of Langemarck; a rather inconsequential pile of rubble on high ground which was as unobtainable a goal for the attacking infantry as Antarctica.

He pulled up an overturned shell crate and insisted himself into the circle, thrusting his cold hands over the mean flame, which flickered and spat under the light rain, threatening to extinguish itself at any moment and take the paltry heat along with it.

The soldiers eyed him curiously and then with open contempt when they saw the red gorget tabs on his uniform.

Without preamble, Gurner dove right in. 'I understand you men served under Subaltern Levy?'

The men grunted and glanced furtively at each other.

A short man with a squat face and tangle of dirty tar-black hair answered. 'We were, at that, sir.'

Gurner addressed the man. 'You Corporal Langfoot?'

'Aye, sir.'

'I assume you know what happened to the subaltern?'

'Gone west by his own hand, from what I hear.'

A couple of the men snickered, though Langfoot continued to stare at Gurner with a dour look.

'What can you tell me of him?'

Langfoot grunted and looked around at the men.

'Speaking plainly, sir?'

'Yes.'

'He was a windy lad, sir. Not fit to be an officer, in my humble opinion. And not too keen to take advice. Most of the time he'd hide in his dugout, leave us poor bastards to the fates and our squalid funk holes. And he wasn't too friendly with the rum ration, either.' A number of the men mumbled their consent at the last statement. The boys sure loved their rum ration in the trenches. 'Drank most of it himself, the blasted coward.' He shot Gurner a nervous look. 'If you'll forgive my candour, Captain.'

Gurner nodded. 'Doesn't sound like a popular man.'

Langfoot smiled, showing a row of small, pointy yellow teeth. 'True. He weren't at that.'

Another of the boys spoke up. 'What's this all 'bout, sir? He's dead and all.'

'Dead he is, but his father is a man of some importance, so the brigadier wants an investigation.'

The boy who'd spoken lowered his head and stared into the meagre fire with an unfathomable expression on his face. Gurner couldn't be sure, but he thought the lad was starting to tear up.

He turned back to Langfoot. 'So you think Levy killed himself, because he was scared?'

'Right. Can't say I don't blame him, though. Wipers isn't a place for the faint of heart. Jerry blasts the place with stick bombs, mortars, and rakes it with machine gun fire all the day long. And a man's as likely to drown in the mud as catch a piece of steel. No blighty ones to be had in the salient, sir, it's death and no mistake.'

'Did you know a lad by the name of Turner; Levy's batman?'

Langfoot gritted his teeth. A couple of the men murmured. In the background the shells picked up in intensity, flashing gold on the grey horizon.

'I knew him,' Langfoot said at last.

'What happened to him?'

Langfoot spat. 'Two nights ago, Levy took us out on patrol. Get a look at the Boche wire and see if we couldn't cut some holes in it. Needless to say, things didn't go as planned. Levy got caught in the mud and started hollering to high heaven. If Jerry didn't see us coming, he sure heard us, by God. Turner was killed at this point.'

'Heard he was well liked.'

'He was. Not a friendlier lad in the whole regiment.'

Gurner mulled it over. Whatever had happened to Levy, whether he had killed himself or not, it somehow had to do with Turner. He felt like he was missing a piece of the puzzle.

He stood up to leave.

'Thank you for your help.'

'What you going to tell the brigadier, Captain?'

'Seems pretty conclusive to me,' he said, even though it didn't. 'Levy killed himself.'

Langfoot grinned, yellow teeth flashing. 'And good riddance...that is if I can still speak plain, sir.'

Gurner turned around without responding and walked away from the dying flame.

§

Gurner was trudging through the sludge when he heard someone slogging up behind him.

He turned, his hand dropping to his holster. The boy froze in the glare of the battered horizon and raised his hands slightly. Gurner recognized him as the lad from the fire, who'd had tears in his eyes.

'It's Private Carmichael, sir.'

'Right, Carmichael. What can I do for you, son?'

'Sir, I was hoping to talk to you 'bout Subaltern Levy.'

'Sure thing, but let's get out of this blasted rain, what do you say?'

Carmichael grinned and lowered his hands. 'I'll say so, sir, puts me right off does the rain.'

They found an old hut with a caved in roof and soot-blackened boards. The place had the smell of mildew and the ubiquitous poison gas shells which the Germans lobbed over on a daily basis.

Gurner lit a nub of candle and set it on a rotted chest covered with blackish mould.

'What can I for you, son?' he asked.

The boy took off his helmet and ran his hands through his spiky dull hair.

'Corporal Langfoot was wrong to speak that way 'bout the Sub, sir. He may have put on some airs, but he was a decent bloke.'

'You don't think he was windy?'

Carmichael nervously tapped his knees. 'Think we're all bit windy, sir. Exceptin' the corporal. Not much seems to faze the old dog.'

Gurner thought about Langfoot. While he wouldn't go as far as to call him a suspect, the man definitely left a foul taste in his mouth.

'What do you know about the corporal, Carmichael?'

'The Corp? He's been out here a while, bit too long I'd wager. Since Loos, or so I've heard. Got himself a bellyful of shrapnel on the Somme.'

Gurner grunted. He could commiserate; he'd caught a bit of shrapnel himself out near Gommecourt. Got a wound stripe for his efforts and two-months back in dear old blighty. Still he was luckier than most. He'd had a friend in the trenches that'd caught a piece of shrapnel in his arm, no more than a pinprick. Boy was grinning from ear-to-ear at his luck. Two days later he was dead from septicaemia. The reaper didn't keep to any set rules in northern France; his scythe fell indiscriminate.

'Do you know what the corporal did before the war?' Gurner asked.

Carmichael smiled. 'Spent some time in prison, from what I hear. Don't like to speak on himself too much.'

Gurner leaned forward. The move made Carmichael nervous and he leaned back. 'Do you know what happened out there on patrol, Carmichael? What happened to Turner?'

Carmichael looked down at his feet and started kneading his hands together, the scrub of candle flickering across his tortured face.

'Took a bullet from old Jerry, sir, what I heard. I wasn't there, so I couldn't rightly say.'

'But you were there when they got back, right?'

'Aye, sir. They all made it back, exceptin' Turner. And McGillis was all shot up.'

'What happened to McGillis?'

Carmichael grimaced. 'The stretcher bearers sent him down to the Casualty Clearing Station at Remy Siding. I've seen a lot of men wounded, Captain, I don't think he made it.'

'What happened when they made it back?'

'Langfoot was raging mad 'bout something, cursing and yelling at Mr. Levy. Levy was real angry 'bout it too; said he was going to see to it that Langfoot got punished for his actions. Langfoot just kept screaming 'bout Turner.'

'Were Turner and Langfoot friends?'

Carmichael still didn't look up. 'Aye, sir. They was the best of chums. Came out together.'

'Did Turner get along with Subaltern Levy?'

Now he looked up. His eyes went wide, candlelight glistening across the wetness at the corners.

'They didn't always see eye to eye, guess you could say.'

Gurner nodded and gestured for the boy to continue.

'Er...Mr. Levy wasn't always keen on taking advice, sir.'

'And that grated with Langfoot and Turner?'

'Aye.'

'All right then, son.' Gurner stood up. 'Best o' luck in the coming push.' He held out his hand.

Carmichael stood up and shook it.

§

Gurner bounced atop his charger. None too fine a horseman before the war, it was a particular mercy he wasn't thrown from the saddle, given the deplorable state of the roads. The horse, as if sensing his trepidation, whickered its contempt the entire way to Etaples. A two-day ride that left him bruised and saddle-sore.

The adjutant had managed to find out where they'd sent McGillis. The Jock was still alive and had been sent to the hospital at Etaples, though the orderly the adjutant had screamed at on the blower sounded none to convinced that the lad would survive much longer.

The adjutant, taking his cue from the brigadier, had insisted Gurner make haste to Etaples right away, and had 'kindly' loaned him his personal chestnut bay for the journey.

The scene at the hospital was one of chaos. The casualties from the Ypres offensive were arriving by the trainload. The nursing sisters had their hands full, so Gurner didn't take offense when his initial queries were met with caustic responses and perfunctory dismissals.

After several hours of waiting and trying to ignore the pitiable cries of the wounded, he was directed to a cot in the north wing of the ward, where the worst cases were made comfortable.

At first Gurner thought he was too late. McGillis lay on the bed with his deep blue eyes open and glassy, staring at the raftered ceiling. But a moment later he blinked and glanced at Gurner.

'How goes it, Jock?' Gurner asked as he took a seat beside the cot.

McGillis took a wheezing breath, his heavily bandaged chest rising tremulously. 'Jerry got me this time, Captain, I'm done.'

'I'm sure you'll pull through, lad,' Gurner said, trying to sound cheerful but failing miserably.

McGillis took another belaboured breath then stared back up at the ceiling, his eyes losing focus and his lips trembling.

Gurner leaned forward and laid his hand gently on the soldier's arm. 'Son? Can you hear me? Son?'

McGillis coughed violently, dribbles of blood rolling down his chin. 'Aye, sir.'

'Good lad.'

Gurner lowered his head, trying to block out the plaintive cries of the wounded. In the next bed over a Tommy was wrapped from head to waist in splotched linen, and was muttering incoherently, calling for his mum it sounded like.

'McGillis,' Gurner started, his voice thick. 'I understand you were on the patrol where Private Turner was killed.'

McGillis groaned, his mouth twisting into a pained rictus. 'Aye, sir. Levy shot him.'

Gurner was stunned. 'What's that, lad?'

McGillis started gasping for air. 'Shot...shot him, sir. He wanted to go back, but Levy was determined, shot him right through the heart, he d-did.'

'He executed his own man?' Gurner asked.

'Aye, called Turner a coward. The corporal was livid.'

Suddenly McGillis' eyes went wide and his body was racked with hard coughs, red froth issuing from his lips.

Gurner jumped out of his chair. 'Nurse! Nurse!' He looked around desperately. A nursing sister came racing over and bent over McGillis as the heavy coughs continued to harass his body, pressing a stethoscope to his chest.

She looked over at Gurner and shook her head solemnly.

After a moment McGillis lay still. The nurse closed his eyes and shuffled off without so much as another word.

Gurner stood transfixed staring at the corpse of the young lad. He'd seen plenty of death in his times in the trenches and spent in hospital, but it never ceased to shock him.

Two orderlies came over and unceremoniously dumped McGillis on a stretcher, and started carrying him away.

'Just like that?' Gurner asked, staring daggers at the orderlies.

One of the orderlies gave him a sad smile. 'Need the bed, Captain.'

§

Gurner picked his way through the crowded trenches. The Royal Warwicks had attacked the previous day and the details were sketchy. It wasn't even known if they'd carried the shattered town of Langemarck.

The stench was overpowering, a mixture of death and poison gas. The front-line trench was clogged with dead bodies and wounded troops. Occasionally he gave a wounded Tommy a cigarette.

The brigadier had insisted he find the Royal Warwicks and get to the bottom of the mystery surrounding Subaltern Levy's death. The fact that the Warwicks were in the midst of an attack was of no importance to the brigadier.

His mind still reeled from what McGillis had told him in the hospital. He'd heard rumours of men who'd been executed in the line for insubordination, but to have one of those stories actually confirmed was another matter entirely.

A runner ran past, covered in sickly green mud.

'How goes it,' Gurner called.

'It's a bloody swamp,' the runner growled in response, not even slowing down.

A soldier sat on the fire step a cigarette dangling from shaking fingers, a bloodied bandage wrapped round his head.

'Can you direct me to the Warwicks?' Gurner asked.

The soldier laughed humourlessly. 'You're looking at 'em, sir. What's left of 'em anyway.'

Gurner glanced around at the thriving mass of wounded and dying. Shells continued to fall thickly, sending up plumes of rotten mud. A machine gun raked the parapet, causing him to flinch.

He glanced back at the wounded soldier. He could just make out the soldiers tarnished cap badge--the white antelope with a coronet wrapped around its neck, the regimental insignia of the Royal Warwickshire Regiment.

'What happened?' he asked.

'It was a massacre, sir. Mud waist deep, and high-explosive shells to boot. Not to mention the god-awful snipers. They're sure energetic.'

'Did any make it to their targets?'

'A couple maybe. They'd be holed up in those pillboxes, I suppose.'

Gurner stood on the fire step and gingerly poked his head over the parapet. No man's land was indeed a swamp, everywhere were shell-holes and bodies in all states of decomposition. In the distance he saw the grey rise of a pillbox, briefly glimmering in and out of sight in the soupy fog. He wondered if he shouldn't just tell the brigadier he couldn't find the Warwicks and be done with it, but he knew the old man wouldn't go for it. The bloody donkey wouldn't be happy until he'd seen Gurner gone west.

Gurner groaned. With nervous fingers he pulled out his flask and took a long draught of rum.

'Nip across fast, sir,' the soldier said. 'Even with the fog, Jerry can hear you. Be jolly careful.'

'I will at that, thank you.' He tossed the half-full flask at the soldier. The soldier caught it and smiled up at him, nodding his thanks.

He waited until the machine gun had traversed the parapet and went over the top. The visibility was poor, but he could see the muzzle flash of the German machine guns and hear the wicked snap and hiss of the bullets as they cut through the air, bare inches away.

He bent over as much as possible, his breath coming fast and ragged. The mud grabbed at his gum boots and his legs were straining from the effort. It was impossible to move faster than a crawl through the heavy mud and he had to constantly hide behind corpses and in shell-holes to avoid the flying shrapnel and withering machine gun fire.

A soldier started yelling at him as he neared the pillbox.

He ran up to it and flopped down against its bullet-riddled face, amazed that he hadn't been hit.

A dirty face poked through the firing slit. 'Sir, you have to move fast through the opening, Jerry's got it pegged. Move fast or he's bound to get you.'

Gurner nodded. He took a couple deep breaths and ran around the side of the pillbox, kicking over tins and reels of wire and leaping over bodies, some in field gray, some in khaki.

He dived through the curtained opening as the bullets crackled against the concrete.

The room was dark and crowded with men, many of them wounded. Cigarette smoke billowed around the ceiling making it hard to breathe.

He recognized Captain Greenfoss. The man was sitting on a bunk, next to a German soldier, who had his leg off at the knee and was begging for Greenfoss to kill him.

Greenfoss smiled when he saw Gurner walk over. He stood up and they shook hands.

'Nice to see you made it, Captain,' Greenfoss said. 'We were taking bets as to whether or not you'd make it through the barrage.'

Gurner smiled despite himself. 'Hope you didn't lose too many francs.'

Greenfoss shrugged. 'Who's to say I'd have gotten a chance to spend them, anyway.'

'What's the situation?' Gurner asked.

'We're just waiting at this point. I haven't got a dozen men left in the whole company. I've sent three runners back to the colonel for orders, but none of them have made it back.'

It was probably a good thing, Gurner thought; the colonel had explicit orders from the brigadier to press the attack at all costs.

'Well, sit tight for now,' he said.

Greenfoss smiled. 'You don't have to tell me twice.'

Gurner sat down on the bunk, catching his breath.

'Any of Levy's old section make it?' he asked.

'Still with that, eh?'

'Still.'

Greenfoss stood up and looked around the cramped pillbox. 'Carmichael,' he shouted. 'Is that you over there, lad?'

'Aye,' a shaky voice called.

Gurner walked towards the sound of the voice. Carmichael was lying on a dirty stretcher, his uniform gummed with mud. His hands were wrapped around his stomach.

Gurner knelt down beside him. 'They get you, son?'

'Aye, sir,' Carmichael croaked.

'Can I get you anything?'

'I could do with a smoke, sir.'

Gurner placed a cigarette between the boys lips and lit it. Carmichael puffed on it greedily. 'Thanks.'

'Don't mention it.' Gurner took off his helmet and ran his hand through his hair. 'Did anyone else in your section make it?'

Carmichael shook his head. 'They all got it, sir. The corporal took one through the head, before he even made it over the parapet.'

'Sorry to hear that.' He hated the brigadier for making him do this. 'So, I talked to McGillis.'

Carmichael eyed him warily. 'How's he getting on?'

'He, uh...didn't make it.'

Carmichael nodded.

'So, look. He told me Levy shot Turner. You know anything about that?'

Carmichael grimaced. 'That he did, sir. From what I heard.'

'I imagine Corporal Langfoot was pretty upset.'

'He was, sir, he was.'

Gurner leaned forward. 'Tell me what happened, son.'

Carmichael shakily pulled the cigarette from his lips with bloodied fingers. When he spoke his voice was low, barely above a whisper. 'Langfoot was mad with rage, sir. Callin' the subaltern a coward and a murderer. He went to talk to the subaltern. Me and a couple of the other lads guarded the entrance to the dugout while he went down. Next thing I knew I heard a lot of yelling and then a gunshot. Langfoot came up a minute later smiling, saying he got the bastard. I swear, sir, I didn't know what he was planning.'

Gurner nodded. 'I believe you, son, I believe you.'

'What are you going to do, sir? I mean...everyone's dead. Excepting me. And I imagine I'll be following pretty soon here.'

Gurner leaned back and placed his head in his hands. 'I don't know.' The boy was right. Even if Levy shot Turner and then Langfoot shot Levy, what difference did it make now? Everyone was dead. But still, he didn't want the boy's family thinking he'd committed suicide.

'I just don't know.'

After a moment he looked back at Carmichael, but the lad was dead.

§

Gurner stood before the brigadier. His uniform was dirty and he was so tired he could barely stand. The old man kept him waiting, pontifically shuffling papers on his desk. After a moment he poured himself a whiskey. Then he poured a second and slid it across the desk, gesturing to Gurner.

He was surprised but he gulped it down.

'Thank you, sir.'

The brigadier waved it away. 'So what have you got for me, Captain? Did you find out how Levy was killed?'

'I did, sir.'

The brigadier waited patiently, hands clasped around his glass.

Gurner took a deep breath. 'He was killed in action, sir.'

'Was he?'

'Yes, sir.'

The brigadier nodded and dismissed him. Gurner walked out of the chateau and onto the rubble strewn roads of Poperinghe.

In the distance the shells continued to fall, grinding Flanders into an impenetrable wasteland and lighting up the horizon.

William Knight lives and writes in Upstate New York. He is currently pursuing a degree in European History, with a mind towards teaching. His work has appeared in *Electric Velocipede, Space and Time,* and *Necrotic Tissue,* among others. He maintains an irregularly updated blog over at www.williamknight1.blogspot.com.

In Cappadocia

by AshleyRose Sullivan

We have arrived in Cappadocia and we see nothing but dry hills. The people there are hidden, the general said. Dark and invisible against the night—they blur into the caves. Their bodies turn to rock and their voices to sand and their whispers creep into our ears as we walk alongside our armoured mares, too nervous and skittish to carry us.

As we march, my father's spear grows heavy in my hand. Unfamiliar stars shine above us and reflect pale silver light in the bronze of our shields. In our ears, there is a thumping. It is only the sound of us. Leather rubbing leather, brass ornaments tinkling on saddles and reins, worn boots in the grit, our footsteps uneven and unsure. Our breath is coarse and thin with fear and we all know we are walking into a ghost town. A ghost country.

Formations of rock, shaped like cloaked figures, tower above us. Their shadows are lined with moonlight as they stand sentinel over what lies below. Carved into the ground beneath us is a vast hidden honeycomb of cities. We have been told that the earth hides a subterranean civilization of armed men, their teeth and swords gleaming and sharp.

A hiss of fearful whispers creeps through our regiment. The men below are monsters. They dig into the ground with clawed hands. They kneel at the foot of a strange stone cross, worshiping a deity once dead, then alive. Their soldiers are waiting. Waiting with a thousand ways to slice great and silent stripes into our throats.

When a silver cloud crosses the moon, the light changes and we can see the seemingly shifting, shadowed entrances in the cliff face. In an instant, I think I see the sparkle of eyes or metal or both but then it is gone. Dust blows from the tall stone towers, these unnatural formations of rock, and I breathe it in. It burns my lungs and I imagine this land is cursed or poisoned by the monsters below.

I walk and feel the sand shift under my feet and I jump. It is only sand. My tongue is a dry lump inside the hollow of my head. It scratches against the ridges at the top of my mouth and feels like old, cracked hide.

They are watching even now. I feel their eyes on me, cave dark and gleaming like pearls. I can smell the nervous metallic sweat of my comrades, dripping off their shoulders and down their arms.

Steam rises from little holes in the ground. Are they chimneys? As I move closer, I imagine that the steam smells of burnt flesh, of blood, of red liquid metal. Droplets of vapour settle on my eyelashes. I sniff. The scent is only yeast and grain.

I ache from within. I stand above the city and I crave the bread I smell baking inside the ground. There are rumours that the city below holds twenty levels, that it is fifty-thousand strong, that wine and olive oil and cheese and children are all made beneath the earth in echoing violet darkness. These cannot be men. Only animals raise their young underground. My own wine, my own bread, my own children were made under the stars. I ache for those stars. I ache for the cool of my home and the dirt of my roads.

It is too hot and this place is an impossible fairy kingdom and as my horse strikes the ground with his hooves, a cloud of thin dust rises. I feel the spear in my hand, the pads below my fingers, hard and callused. Once I used these hands to form great red pots. I kneel and lay my palm to the ground. A musical vibration travels through my fingertips. They are marching. Or, they are dancing.

AshleyRose Sullivan has an MFA in Creative Writing from Spalding University and a BS in Anthropology from Northern Kentucky University. Some of her fiction has appeared in *Word Riot* and *Wigleaf* and her short story, 'How To Make A Stunt Man', published in the *Medulla Review*, was recently adapted into a musical. She writes and lives here and there with her husband Scott and their many imaginary friends.

The Orchid Hunters

by Priya Sharma

July 27th 1892

I wrote to Kitty again today. Marcus raised an eyebrow at me as I handed the letter to the first mate. He's so trusting of the natives but not our fellow Englishmen. When I pressed him on the point he muttered something about colonial savages and I pretended not to understand his meaning.

It pains me to admit that Marcus is correct. Captain Dawkins of The Liberty is a prime example. He is the colour of mahogany and it makes him appear dirty. He's slovenly and eyes the half naked native women. I despair. We are among the ungodly and the fallen and all because of a damned flower.

August 1st 1892

The town's chaplain met the steamer on the jetty. I am no religious zealot. Christianity is an English duty that should be practiced with English moderation. Still, I am relieved to be met by a man of the cloth, even if he is a Welsh one. When I said as such to Marcus he became very cold with me.

August 2nd 1892

The chaplain and his wife held a dinner this evening in our honour. It was attended by some desperate looking missionaries and our own Captain Dawkins of The Liberty.

'An orchid?' Our host was incredulous.

Out here, in darkest Africa, there was no way he could know that orchids have set the English gentry aflame.

'At the request of Lord Huntley of Cheshire.'

Maria, the servant, spilt some wine upon the tablecloth. The chaplain chided her. There was perspiration on her neck and one of the buttons on her uniform was missing.

'Are orchids so dangerous that it requires two of you?' The chaplain's wife was sharp. The rest of the company tittered nervously. She must rule them with an iron rod.

Marcus was engaged in chewing the tough fowl before us, so I explained.

'Lord Huntley thought it prudent to send a pair of men for a greater chance of success. It's perilous out here, among the snakes and crocodiles.'

'A costly venture.'

I ignored this vulgarity from Dawkins. My ambitions are finer than that.

The chaplain's wife leant forward, having spied an opportunity. Her small black eyes flitted between Marcus and myself, unsure of where to settle.

'I think we may be of help to you.'

'How so?'

'You'll encounter several different tribes in the interior. You'll need a guide who knows their languages, as well as the geography. We have a man who'd be perfect.'

'I don't think so.' I wasn't keen to be in her debt.

'Hold on,' Marcus cut across me. 'Tell me more.'

I was furious that he saw fit to contradict me but I bit my tongue, not wanting to draw more attention to it.

'Oliver's a native. We took him in when his parents died. He's strong and his English is excellent.'

'He's a fine shot too,' her husband added.

'He's so useful to us,' she continued. 'He'd be difficult to spare. He's almost like a son.'

I doubt her breast harbours anything that might pass for maternal feeling.

'We'd compensate you for his time.'

I wanted to kick Marcus under the table for that. The woman didn't look at me again, deferring to Marcus in everything for the rest of the evening.

Marcus and I sat on the veranda after the others had gone to bed. Our cigar smoke filled the pools of lamp light. He ignored my anger at his behaviour over dinner.

'So Philip, is she worth all this?' His cigar glowed as he sucked on it.

Damned impertinence. He was referring to Kitty. I suppose the time for correcting him is long past. My father was too generous with him, more than owing to the orphaned nephew of my governess, and now Marcus is accustomed to taking liberties. Marcus left for South Africa with a gold expedition when I was in my final year at Eton. Since his return to Carfax we are over familiar strangers and he ignores my attempts to put our relationship on a proper footing. My father's dying wish was that our governess, and Marcus after her, have lifelong use of a cottage by the river at Carfax. I can never wholly be rid of him.

'Well, I suppose you must do something to distinguish yourself from Kitty's other admirers but there are far easier quests she could have sent you on.'

'How dare you. She is devoted to her father's happiness. I can only hope she will be as devoted to mine.'

'Indeed,' he replied with a smirk.

I have always found orchids faintly indecent. That Lord Huntley pursues them with such passion disconcerts me. My own father was for the manly occupations of hunting and fishing. To be embroiled in Huntley's scheme for botanical glory is too ridiculous.

We smoked in silence. The river was below us, its movements so languid that it was almost motionless. Ripples fanned out on its surface, a sinuous curve sliding on the water as if on oil and then it was gone.

August 3rd 1892

We make plans for the interior. I hope Marcus is as good as Huntley thinks or how else are we to find the damn thing?

Marcus is an odd sort. He pretends to care for nothing but something distasteful happened earlier. We were walking in the grove and came upon Dawkins who had the servant girl, Maria, against a tree. He had her by the throat, his other hand fumbling with his breeches. I turned away, not seeing that it was my business that Dawkins had fallen so low as to consort with servants but Marcus had already pressed his pistol to Dawkins' temple.

'Put her down.'

Dawkins spat at Marcus. Tobacco stained spittle landed on his cheek. I'd have blown his brains out for that.

'Put her down,' Marcus repeated. 'What makes you think you have the right?'

Dawkins' head was bowed with the pressure of the barrel tip. When he released Maria, Marcus struck him with the pistol butt, bloodying his noise.

We walked away in silence. Marcus set his lips in a thin line when he looked at me, as if I were the one with some girl against a tree and not the captain.

August 4th 1892

Last night I dreamt I was with Maria. My head was between her breasts. This damn country is infecting me.

August 15th 1892

We have made camp. Marcus has given me his word that his priority will be Huntley's elephant orchids, although he is collecting others. From what Marcus has intimated he did well in his South African gold venture but is keen to try botany, where there is fame and money to be had. As a boy he was always outdoors with his notebooks, annotating his sketches in Latin.

Marcus spends much of his time with the chaplain's foundling, Oliver. He's our interpreter but Marcus has asked him to teach him some of the language. They always have their heads together as though they're kindred spirits. I'm glad no-one else is here to see it.

I called Oliver over to ask him how far we had to travel to the orchids.

'My name is Melingwa.'

He laboured each syllable as though talking to an idiot. I ignored his ungratefulness at being blessed enough receive a proper Christian name.

I miss Kitty. I remember how gracious she was when I brought her mundane tea roses. We stood in her father's conservatory surrounded by rare blooms. Her waist is a mere hand span.

August 16th 1892

This climate is stifling. The humidity is terrible. My shirt is perpetually damp.

I had the watercolour of the Elephant Orchid propped up before me as I shaved this morning. It's a study from the Royal Society's collection, taken before it died. I was trying to memorise the three petals, each one wrinkled, delicate shades of grey that become a pink flush at its heart.

'Strange, isn't it?' Marcus stood behind me. He has forgone shaving for a beard, which he trims. 'We go west towards the ruins.'

It irritates me that he keeps me informed as an afterthought.

'Are the orchids there?'

'In the graveyard.'

'What?'

'An elephant graveyard.' He grinned. 'Everyone's assumed the natives call it the Elephant Orchid because of its looks but no-one's bothered to ask. It grows from elephant skulls. It likes brain matter.'

I pulled a face. The ghoulish flower will be my undoing.

August 20th 1892

I was cleaning my rifle by the fire last night. Marcus had just returned from a sortie. Outside the circle of light, the darkness was full. I saw something that stopped my heart. Two circles reflected the firelight as they blinked at me. I turned the gun on it and took the safety catch off. It made a harsh, metallic sound.

'Philip.' Marcus was at my side, his own gun in hand.

It padded closer, materialising in pieces in the firelight. A face, whiskered and spotted. A broad, powerful chest. Enormous paws. A twitching tail.

'Beautiful.' Marcus had her in his sights but didn't fire.

Oliver said something I didn't understand. His voice was reverence itself.

A growl rumbled from deep inside the beast. Her mouth was full of pointed knives. She shifted her weight from one leg to the other, not settling but not advancing either. I held my breath and waited. Then, as she retreated, I shot her.

Oliver had the audacity to shake his head at me and walk away.

Marcus is a strange man. Willing to kill an English captain but he hasn't spoken to me since I killed the leopard last night.

Later -

The natives have met with Marcus and Oliver. They all squatted down in a ring and talked until dawn, pointing at me from time to time.

Marcus came over, his mouth set in the hard line which I suppose is his way of showing me that I've displeased him. As if I care for his good opinion.

'It's no good. They're leaving.'

'Why?'

'The leopard.'

'That's ridiculous.'

'What the blazes do you think they have tattooed on their chests? It's the tribe spirit. She was a good omen and you shot her.'

I suppose the squared toothed creature does look a little like a cat.

August 21st 1892

We now only have Oliver to direct us and he's not as familiar with this region as the leopard tribe. As they departed, Marcus asked me for a second time if I wouldn't go with them.

'I'm coming with you.'

'It might be easier if you didn't.'

There it was. He thinks I'm a liability.

'Nonsense. You'll need an extra pair of eyes and gun.'

I won't let him take all the glory.

We set off, leaving the leopard carcass, eyes thick with flies. The natives refused to carry her back to the mission for me.

I had to stop after a few miles. Marcus emptied out everything unnecessary from my pack. I hid this journal and pencil in my pocket.

August 22nd 1892

I thought, wrongly, that the discipline and cruelty of Eton had prepared me for everything. Marcus gave me his spare bootlaces when mine snapped. When he saw my blistered feet, he insisted we make camp and produced a bottle of iodine. Oliver went off in search of food, an attempt to augment our rations.

'Do you regret coming?' I asked Marcus.

'No. Your father would never have forgiven me if I'd let you do this alone.'

The fire crackled. We sat facing each other, our feet up on the log on which we perched. It was as if we were boys back in the nursery and I felt a companionship that I hadn't known for years.

It seems to me that Father did Marcus a grave disservice. He doesn't know his place in the world. He is neither master nor servant.

August 24th 1892

My wild dreams shame me. Kitty crawled towards me on all fours, emerging from the darkness. She licked her lips, moving constantly, like the leopard. When she finally stood up, she was naked and I pushed her against a tree. My hand was on her throat. Her hips made rhythmic motions to an unseen drum. She opened her mouth and inside there was an elephant orchid, in delicate shades of pink and grey. It opened itself to me, quivering with dew.

I was moaning. Her hands were on my chest and I tried to move them downwards. She fought me off.

Philip, wake up, for God's sake.' It was Marcus, shaking me awake. 'Stop that bloody racket.'

Marcus didn't notice my flushed cheeks. He was too concerned with the drums, which weren't a figment of my dream at all but very real and very close.

August 27th 1892

Oliver could have run away many times but has shown his mettle and stayed. He has great respect for Marcus, who calls him Melingwa.

They were talking quietly, thinking I couldn't hear. I overheard Marcus say to him, 'If anything should happen to me, will you take care of Philip? Make sure he gets back home. Promise me.'

The African nodded slowly. I resent being treated like an imbecile.

Oliver thinks he can get us to the city. The leopard tribe warned him to avoid the drums at all costs. We have skirted the source of the sound. It is perpetual and maddening.

August 1892 (exact date unknown)

I can't believe we are here. It is an awful, empty place of huge stone steps and altars. Oliver is keeping watch from the wall. The drumming is getting fainter.

I have a fever and am sweating profusely. The dreams are unrelenting. I am ashamed to write down the things I do to Kitty. If I ever get home, I fear I shall be no fit husband.

We are sheltering under an arched doorway, afraid to light a fire. The hanging vines look like serpents. Great, heady scented blooms burst from the mouths of toppled idols and consume crumpling parapets.

'They were a great nation once.'

I snorted.

'These men were kings, Philip.'

'Heathens and savages.' I was being deliberately obtuse.

'Someone will say the same of us one day. We all presume to be the pinnacle of civilisation. Rome fell. Spain fell. So will Britannia.'

'Rot.'

I don't care for his philosophy, even though we are sat in the ruins of the evidence.

August 1892

We have found it. I have held the Elephant Orchid in my hand and wondered at the fragility of the thing that brought me half way around the world.

The elephant graveyard is on the far side of the city where the defensive wall has crumbled. I have never seen such a place. A cemetery for monoliths. It is littered with a dozen carcasses in various states of decay. The smell is foul. Torn hides hang loosely from rotting flesh. There are gleaming bones, a fortune in ivory curving from bare skulls.

We saw the damndest thing. When we arrived there were visitors. Marcus explained they were migrating herd. It was as if they were passing by and thought they'd pay their respects. They trumpeted in outrage and stamped their feet, scattering the greedy vultures. The ugly birds hovered at a safe vantage point.

The elephants paid attention to a single skeleton that had long since been picked clean. They each caressed it with their trunks, lingering as though bidding goodbye to an old friend. Finally the bull turned and the others followed, a solemn line with their heads bowed.

'Isn't it strange?'

'Why? They have family bonds, just as we do, Philip. They know love and loyalty. They mourn their own.'

We'd been well informed about the orchids, which grew from ear and eye sockets, from holes caved in the skulls. Any way to penetrate the precious brain.

Marcus showed me how to pack them for transport but I'm ashamed to confess to retching so badly that Marcus had to finish the task for me.

In the end we could only find ten plants that were healthy enough to travel. I pray this is enough.

September 1892

It's a miracle. We have been rescued by The Liberty. I never thought I'd be pleased to see Dawkins or him us, especially as the last time we saw him he was at the end of Marcus' gun barrel.

But I get ahead of myself.

We traced our way back to the city gates. I'm shamed to admit I'd expected Oliver to have run away but he was waiting on the wall with his rifle primed. Next to us, he no longer looked like a savage.

We were weary but in good spirits. I felt, for the first time, an appreciation of Africa. It seemed utterly foreign and grand, shafts of sunlight piercing the towering canopy. Birds, in brazen reds and blues, squawked and wheeled over our heads. I stopped and stared, seeing it with happier eyes. It wasn't until Oliver came racing back through the undergrowth towards us that I realised that something was wrong. He motioned for us to hide. There were no beating drums to warn us, only the sounds of the living, breathing jungle.

The men that led the procession were made of muscles and sinew. That they were warriors was as much in the way they moved as in the spears they carried. The group was thirty strong. Six of them bore their queen aloft. She was magnificent. A giantess. A diadem winked from her forehead and she wore a cape of iridescent plumes. This was no blessed, benign monarch. Her chin was caked in dried blood. Her eyes blazed with unholy fire and I drew back, afraid she'd seen me. I tremble to recall her.

Behind her, trussed and carried on a pole, was one of the tribe of leopard men who'd been our guides. His head lolled. I hope he was dead. It was a hideous sight, meat carved from his oozing thighs and calves as if they'd snacked upon him.

The only drumming was their feet as they passed by.

We tried to stay clear of them but they seemed to change path frequently, forcing us in new directions. Even Oliver became disorientated, unsure of the direction home. Each rustle and snap in the undergrowth became a torture. The devils made sport with us, drumming for days at a time as if they disdained sleep. They drove us ahead of them, making us march without pause and I thought exhaustion would kill me. If I dared to close my eyes, all I could see were those terrible eyes and bloodstained teeth.

The splendour I'd glimpsed now mocked me. My arms ached from hacking at the dense vegetation. In the darkness of the canopy, I hungered for the sunlit fields and copses of Carfax.

I mused over their hesitation at attacking. Oliver gave me a sour look. 'They're seasoning the meat.'

The drums started up again. A sudden sound that startled me. I wanted to fall to the ground and give up but Oliver pushed me on. The faster we ran, the faster the drumming became. My heart couldn't keep up. I thought it would stop.

Then silence, filled by something else. The sound of the river. So here was our dilemma. We would be strung upon a pole or have to take our chances in the water.

As we ran, we heard another sound being carried downstream. A determined chugging, the mechanised glory of civilisation steaming towards us. There was a hoot as she took the bend. It was strange fortune that brought us to that point, with The Liberty bearing down on us.

We were giddy at the prospect of salvation, terrified that it would pass us by. We threw away caution, firing our guns and waving our ragged shirts above our heads. What a sight we must have been.

Hearing the steamer, our pursuers broke cover. Their howls froze my blood. The Liberty gave us the cover of her rifles as we ran for the gang plank.

Only two orchids had survived our flight from the city. Mine tipped from its bag. I went back to where it lay as soon as I realised. Marcus, seeing I was no longer at his side, glanced over his shoulder, eyes wide. He shouted my name. One of the warriors ran towards me, spear raised.

Oliver, too, had doubled back. I fancied I could hear their pistols above all the others from the boat. Marcus fired again and a bullet exploded in the chest of my attacker. Too late, too late. As Marcus stood over me, the spear struck him in the thigh and he crumpled to the ground.

Dawkins fired his cannon from the deck. It was a thunder crack that silenced the world. The soft rain of arrows paused for a moment and Marcus, ever level headed, even when wounded, cried and clutched at the spear, 'Just pull it out!'

He was right. The shaft was at least three feet long and it would have been impossible to move him with it stuck in place. There was no time for delicate extraction. Oliver wrenched it free and I tried to staunch the bleeding. Apparently the canon fired again, but I didn't hear it, being so intent on carrying Marcus, who was now unconscious, aboard.

The orchid lay where I'd dropped it.

September 29th 1892

Dawkins has confined us to one cabin. Oliver is allowed in daily to tend to Marcus. He brings me fresh water and fusses over us until the first mate twists his arm and forces him to leave. I'm too weak to write much. My fever rages and abates by turns. What I thought was the fatigue of overexertion is illness.

Marcus is all noise. I am kept awake by my stomach cramps and Marcus' ravings. Although he is pale, his wound is black and smells rank.

I fear neither Marcus nor the single orchid that remains will see England.

September 30th 1892

I am burning. Despite Oliver's protest that I should sleep, I write to preserve my sanity. Marcus, in his delirium, called me, 'My dear brother.'

Brother. He was always the brighter one. Quicker in everything. I remember our father clapping us both on the shoulder. His pride in Marcus' achievements, which always exceeded mine. How Father must've wished that Marcus had been the legitimate one, not I.

My father brought his doxy and his bastard into our home, masquerading as governess and nephew, my mother not yet cold.

I must stop. I think I will be sick.

October 1892

Kitty, Carfax and England are a dream. I am in hell.

I awoke earlier to find Dawkins holding a cup of water to my mouth. My journal was on his knee. When I asked for Oliver he replied, 'Don't concern yourself with him. He's quite safe.'

Dawkins mopped my brow, the cloth sopping with sweat. The orchid withered on the nightstand beside me. He asked me its worth and when I told him, he gave a low whistle.

'It's a pity, especially when you've been to so much trouble to get it.'

Then he said something I didn't quite catch. 'He's going to die anyway.' He must have meant, *it's* going to die, but I can't be sure.

1893

It's strange to read these words again, the Elephant Orchid beside me, now in bloom. It is the only one of its kind in England and has shown itself to be strangely robust. It shouldn't have survived so long. When it dies, a part of me will die too.

I am compelled to account for myself. I don't expect forgiveness. Carfax has been stripped to pay off Dawkins. I've taken to burning the furniture for warmth. The minister comes each day and we pray together but nothing will save my soul.

I am procrastinating. I have a story to finish. I remember fragments of that time aboard The Liberty. I was so weak and feverish. Oliver wasn't allowed near us. Dawkins visited regularly, solicitous for our health but I could see avarice in his eyes. I told him flatly that Lord Huntley wouldn't deal with him. That my safe return, as his future son-in-law, was as important to him as any orchid. A bluff. He wouldn't give a fig who delivered his precious orchid to him. I knew Kitty's tears would be transient and I was proven right. I met her, once, to break things off. Only a few months later her engagement was announced in The Times. So much lost for a woman not worth the having.

Dawkins knelt beside me and put his mouth to my ear, taunting me with secrets from my journal.

'Your brother took that wound for you, you milk-fed sop. He was the better man. There's no doubt of that. What would your father think of you now?'

He would go on in this way and suddenly turn it all about.

'That bastard, Marcus. He has no claim on you. He's just a servant's son. How dare he presume?'

And then it would be, 'We'll not make it to the surgeon in time to save him. It's cruel to let him suffer. They're dying, him and the plant. If he was one of your prize hunters, wouldn't you show him mercy? '

I was on fire. My fever was at its peak. Dawkins goaded me. Confused me. He fuelled my anger. Brother. Brother. Brother. How long had Marcus known?

Dawkins clamped his hands around mine to keep the pistol from falling. I couldn't pull away. Or perhaps I didn't try. Dawkins put the tip of the barrel to Marcus' head. I don't remember what I said, but suddenly the gun was smoking in my hand, having dispensed anger and mercy all at once. Both my finger and Dawkins' were on the trigger. I think that was it. I think so. Oliver was hammering at the door. I heard his protests as they dragged him away.

Marcus was slow to die. He said my name. There was such satisfaction on Dawkins' face. He didn't care for Marcus, even before the incident with the serving girl.

Marcus. Even in that sickened, strickened state, I knew I'd been a party to an awful thing. As he said my name I knew what I'd lost. As a child, he'd picked me up whenever I fell. He read to me. He took the blame and a beating on my behalf more than once. He was the only one who could console me when I cried. He was my brother.

There, the truth. But not the worst of it.

I fainted when Dawkins hacked his head off with a machete.

§

I keep Marcus close. If Dawkins thought I'd give him up a second time he was mistaken. I don't care about the cost. Huntley and other fellows from the Royal Academy send me begging letters that I've long ceased to open. I couldn't give them the orchid, even if I wanted to. Its roots are too entwined with Marcus' skull.

Dawkins, my blackmailer, doesn't know his luck. He presses me for money, not realising I'd be happy to send us both to the gallows but for the one person I must consider, not sent overboard to the crocodiles as I'd feared.

As I sit staring at the fire, my only friend is beside me. The best friend I could have, in fact. He ensures that I don't forget to eat and is company when I can't stand myself. When I told him the truth he didn't turn away from me. When I told him that he wouldn't like it here he came with me anyway because, he said, he'd made a promise. They call him Black Oliver in the village but I call him by his real name, Melingwa.

Priya Sharma lives in the UK. She has had short stories accepted by a variety of magazines including *Albedo One, On Spec, Fantasy Magazine, Dark Tales, Not One of Us* and *Zahir*. Her story, 'The Bitterness of Apples', appeared in the first issue of *Alt Hist*. More information can be found at www.priyasharmafiction.co.uk

Death in Theatre

by Jessica Wilson

I had hoped my death would be more theatrical.

At least I gave Lincoln that. What could be more theatrical than being killed in the theatre? Granted, my performance was the more thrilling of the two. Still, his death will certainly be remembered as one with a certain amount of dignity.

Not for me, though. It's tragic. Strange how sharp my thoughts are when I can't even move my body. The deep hot ache in my neck has faded, but now I can feel the terrifying numbness in my limbs. I had to have my murderer raise my hands so I could see them; I could not raise them myself. 'Useless, useless,' I said, but those were the last words I could force out. My mind may be clear, but even my mouth isn't working right now. They try to get me to swallow something—water, brandy?—but my throat won't work. Not surprising. I believe they shot a gaping hole through it.

I wish death would come faster. They're rifling through my pockets like I'm already dead. Not that I can feel it. But I saw my diary in their hands. Let them read it. Maybe they will realize why I did it. Why it was worth it.

Though a more dignified death. That would have been better. Better than lying like a sack of grain on some farmer's porch. A farmer who didn't even recognize me. Not even when the news of Lincoln's death finally reached him.

Such a shame.

§

The stage is set. The opening applause resonates through the wood at my back. Sweat makes the handle of the gun slick, but I keep my fingers clenched around it all the same. Call it stage fright. Some might think an actor as experienced as I am no longer feels stage fright, but it isn't so; we simply master it. But I will admit that the stage fright is worse tonight.

Plans to kidnap Lincoln are well and good, but killing him is another matter. I don't want to kill; I'm an actor, not an assassin. But it's necessary. If I kill Lincoln, and if Lewis and George kill Johnson and Seward … well, even without killing General Grant, the Union will collapse. Utter chaos. And the Confederacy will grow strong again. Even the damned Union officers will welcome Confederate government in that sort of chaos.

I still have some time. I know this play well, and the laughter that always accompanies Asa Trenchard's line in Act III will cover the gunshot nicely. It might not be as dramatic, but I'm a practical man too, and I'll need the extra time to get away.

But it means plenty of time for my nerves to fray at the ends. Everything is done; I can't think of a single thing I've forgotten. There's a horse waiting for me behind the theater. Lewis and George know their roles. I even had time to post a letter to my sister. All I can do is wait.

Best to watch. It wouldn't do for Lincoln to leave to relieve himself while I'm sitting here letting sweat cover the gun until it's almost too slick to hold. I need to know exactly where he is when the time comes. I turn quietly until I'm kneeling in front of the peephole I drilled into the door of the box and watch the back of Lincoln's head. I'll have to shift between squatting and kneeling. Wouldn't it just ruin the performance if I let my legs get numb and tripped over the balcony railing?

A play has never seemed so long.

But Harry Hawk is on stage now, and the words are coming out of his mouth: 'Don't know the manners of good society, eh? Well, I guess I know enough to turn you inside out, old gal ...' I rise to my feet and put my hand on the doorknob. The first peal of laughter starts. I can't hesitate now. This is the most important role of my career.

The door slams open. I raise the gun and it doesn't slip despite the sweat. The shot is off too fast for anyone in the box to react, and the splatter of gore makes my stomach turn, but there's no time to stop and retch. Major Rathbone is on his feet faster than I could have imagined and he lunges for me, but my knife is already out--my hands have a will of their own--and my breath catches in my throat as the knife catches in his side. The sound of the knife ripping free of flesh is sickening in the lull as the theatre starts to realize something's wrong. I leap over the balcony and the stage rushes to meet me.

The landing is heavy on my leg, but I don't let it slow me. The actors stare—the whole theatre stares—and I straighten. I shove the bloody knife into the air. '*Sic semper tyrannis!*' I scream, and the Latin shreds my throat but I don't care. This will be the line I am known for. This is my grandest scene.

And I run.

§

But maybe it wasn't worth it after all. It's getting harder to think. But some thoughts are clearer than others. It's hard to focus on the men around me now, gathered and waiting for me to die. My final scene, though, is easy. It's the role I'll be remembered for.

For what? The farm family finally got the news, and Johnson surrendered. The last foothold of the Confederacy lost. And George and Lewis failed. So the Confederacy is crumbling and the Union may have lost its tyrant president, but there are still men to step up and take his place.

So am I an assassin? Just a murderer? Where's the revolution in Lincoln's death? Does it mean anything when the Union will still win?

I have to believe that my ... my last and greatest performance ... wasn't a failure.

Maybe ...

            someone will

                        understand

                                  value

                                        —death

                                                ... of a tyrant

Jessica Wilson is a college senior preparing to graduate and start a career in teaching. She has loved writing stories since the fifth grade and reading for even longer, and hopes to inspire a similar love of both reading and writing in her future students. She is an aspiring author who writes predominantly fantasy, but enjoys branching out into other genres on occasion. This is her first published work of fiction, but she hopes that many more will follow.

The Scarab of Thutmose

by Anna Sykora

'Pharaoh is trashing his room again.' The old servant steadied her wig. 'Fetch Amenhotep, quick.'

As a palace guard marched away, a wig brush flew past him and smashed a vase, scattering lotus flowers and shards. 'May the gods protect Amenhotep,' he muttered, 'or Seti will wreck our country.'

'I won't meet the ambassadors,' Seti shrilled at the servants cowering in his chamber. He kicked an ebony table into the wreck of his gilded, lion-headed bed. 'I'd rather be staked in the desert for wild beasts to devour.' Sinking into the sole surviving chair, he flung a cloth-of-gold shawl over his head, as if to hide from the world.

The guard at his heels, the Head Scribe came waddling down the corridor, his fleshy face creased with concern, his bare breasts bobbing. Shaven-headed Amenhotep wore a long kilt of fine, white linen and his collar glittered with gold.

'Lord of the Two Lands, Eye of Ra,' he soothed, and young Seti uncovered his face. (With his full lips and fine cheekbones he should have been a woman, Amenhotep thought.)

'You close the door and come rub my feet,' the pharaoh commanded. 'My poor head's about to burst.'

Shooing the guard and servants away, the scribe pulled shut the mahogany door. 'My lord,' he chided, 'these fits of fury damage your precious image. What if someone on the staff goes gossiping to the ambassadors?'

'You dare tell *me* how to behave?' Seti caught up a statue of the cat goddess Bastet and brandished it like a club. 'I should have you flung into the Nile this morning, with the rest of the palace garbage. The crocodiles would feast on your fat flesh.'

'You won't do that,' said Amenhotep calmly. 'Without me, how could you govern Egypt?'

'The gods only know, Amy.' Pouting Seti stuck the statue back in its niche. 'You're the only one I trust, since my mother ran off with General Taa. You always know what to do.'

'So why don't you tell me what's bothering you?' The scribe eased himself down on a ripped cushion, popped off Seti's expensive sandals and began massaging his delicate feet.

'Ooh that feels almost as good as dancing.' Seti leaned back in his ivory chair. 'I told you before I'm fed up with my duties. What do I care about snails in the Nile that are wrecking the fishing industry? I just want to dance like a lovely maiden and enjoy life.' Springing up he spread his arms and twirled like a top, his kilt of silk flying up around his slender thighs.

'Indeed you have a gift from the goddess Hathor,' Amenhotep said diplomatically. 'Our lady of pleasure and drunkenness loves you. She has never favoured me, even when I was young and slim.'

Seti wheeled around the room, as if performing a magic spell to make the palace melt away, along with his tedious responsibilities.

Struggling to his feet the scribe applauded. Seti clapped him on his fat rump: 'You look like a scribe, Amy, born to sit cross-legged and paint hieroglyphs on papyrus rolls for hours.' He wiggled his own, narrow hips. 'But I was not born to sit on a throne and fiddle with decisions.'

Amenhotep sighed. 'If only we had the scarab of Thutmose, you would learn wisdom and Egypt would be saved.'

'Saved from what?' Seti demanded.

'From yourself, my lord. You are a man; you are seventeen; but you do not govern Egypt as you should. Your dear father (may he hunt and feast with the gods) would have received the Libyan ambassadors. They want you to marry a princess of their country. They have brought you her painted image.'

'Oh don't speak to me of brides or weddings.' Sinking back in his ivory chair, Seti closed his face in his hands.

'My lord, she seems an intelligent girl,' Amenhotep said hopefully. 'With eyes like a pair of stars and teeth like strings of pearls … If you'd only give a banquet for the Libyans tonight, I think I could arrange for dancers. Wouldn't a veil dance be delightful?'

'As you wish,' said Seti abruptly, a sly look in his almond eyes.

§

That same afternoon, Amenhotep met with the High Priest of the Great God Amun-Ra, who'd petitioned the pharaoh for more tithes. As the sun blazed down they conferred in a shady corner of the palace gardens, sipping dark beer as two naked slaves fanned them.

'Pardon me, Herihor,' the scribe said suddenly. 'I don't believe you voyaged all the way from Memphis to discuss your temple's revenues.'

'The gods have blessed you with wisdom.' Lean, dry and hawk-beaked, the elderly priest already looked mummified. 'Leave us now,' he commanded, and his slaves glided away. Waiting till they were out of earshot he turned again to the scribe: 'We know that for several years you've been seeking the magic scarab of Thutmose. You've studied the palace archives and bought many ancient rolls of papyrus.'

'So I'm interested in archaeology.' The scribe sipped his beer. 'We can learn lessons from the past. We can learn how the great kings governed Egypt.'

'I've reason to believe you've found Thutmose's talisman.'

'Is that so?' Amenhotep popped a honey cake into his mouth. 'This is delicious. Won't you try one? We won't get such cakes in the afterlife.'

Herihor waved the platter away. 'My priesthood has informers everywhere, even on the palace staff. Never fear, I'm offering you a bargain you cannot refuse.'

Amenhotep shot him a piercing glance. 'I can refuse a corrupt bargain.'

'You, who have risen from the mud of the Nile, from a family of barefoot, Delta farmers…'

'It's a matter a million times true, high priest, my name is all my own. I give thanks to the gods for favouring me, and I offer them incense and roast ducks. Still I've worked like a slave to reach this respected position.'

'*My* fathers have handed down the priesthood of Amun-Ra for 11 generations. We have amassed fabulous wealth: more gold than the pharaohs. We'll pay you your ample weight in gold—in coins or ingots, whichever you like—if you give us the scarab of Thutmose.'

'*If* anybody finds it in Egypt, by law it will belong to our pharaoh.'

'Seti is a foolish boy, unable even to govern himself.'

The scribe's lips set in a line firm as the hieroglyph for 'sky.' 'Frankly, high priest, what you are suggesting reeks of treason.'

Raising his chin, Herihor peered down his nose at the uppity commoner: 'You dare to take that tone with me? Great-grandson of a grave-robber!'

'My mother's father made some money in that line, on the side. I've never hidden his blight on my family tree.'

'If you don't cooperate, we have ways to compel your obedience.'

'I serve our pharaoh for the good of Egypt, mother of us all. I have no interest in your gold. More beer?' Without waiting he poured him another cup from the pitcher.

Pushing it away, Herihor scowled as if to strike him dead: 'It has also come to my attention that *you are not what you seem.*'

His hand shaking, Amenhotep set down the cup he'd raised to his lips.

Herihor went on: 'If I accused you of—for example—embezzling funds from the new dam, Seti's guards would arrest you for questioning. They'd make you shed your fine kilt for the ragged loincloth of an accused.' Amenhotep gripped the table's edge, the nails of his hands turning white. 'They'd notice you lack some equipment proper to a man.'

'I am a eunuch,' he said with dignity, 'as everybody knows.'

'No, my dear, you are a *woman*. And women are not allowed to be scribes! Your career has been one long impersonation. You should be flayed and boiled alive.'

'I've served my country and my pharaoh—unlike your priesthood, which serves itself. Never satisfied, you're always wanting more tithes and preying upon our poorest farmers—'

'Don't try to change the subject, scribe. Or should I call you 'missy'? I'm giving you a chance to make a good bargain.'

'You're wasting your life-breath, high priest. If I had the magic scarab here,' (he drew a leather pouch from inside his kilt, and Herihor eyed it hungrily), 'I'd rather be eaten by a crocodile than hand it over to the likes of you. Heed my words, Herihor: someday your greed will destroy you.'

The priest's eyes glinted like a hidden weapon. Without a word he rose and strutted away, snapping his fingers at his slaves to follow.

Amenhotep groaned and wiped the sweat from his forehead. He gulped down the murky beer in his cup and then downed the priest's as well. Leaning back, he patted the rolls of fat on his belly and shut his eyes. Silently he prayed to Isis, the goddess who'd protected him from ruin…

When he opened them, an iridescent feather came spinning down and landed right in his lap. 'That settles it.' He caressed its silky edges and sharp point. 'We can't afford to wait another night.'

§

He'd have to wait though, till after the banquet for the ambassadors that evening. He'd have to wait for the stuffed antelope to be served on platters in the Great Hall, along with fried fish and whole singing birds and sides of tender papyrus-root salad. He'd have to wait for the sweet and sour vegetables, and the dishes of nuts and honey-cakes.

Sweet, murky beer flowed like the Nile in flood. The Libyan ambassadors looked pleased and woozy…

Suddenly a gong resounded, and to the sounds of quick drums and piping a troupe of lovely girls in gauzy veils came whirling into the space between the twin long tables.

Uneasily Amenhotep noticed that the pharaoh had left his place, when protocol required Seti to remain till the banquet's end. Why hadn't he stayed for the dancers he loved? He'd pelt his favourites with gold coins.

But who was this tall and willowy dancer tossing her veils into the air? Alone of the troupe she wore a black silk square concealing half her face. Her lively eyes looked familiar, though lined with black and shaded with green malachite. Rolling her hips and waving her arms, and beating her fine, slender feet in time to the tapping and thudding of the drums, the drums like lovers' hearts beating high, this singularly gifted maiden gathered all the gazes in the Great Hall. Where had he seen her before?

The Libyan ambassadors stood and applauded, tossing her coins as she left the hall. (She let the other dancers scoop them up.) As she undulated past the scribe, she looked him in the eye, as if seeking approval. Then she *winked*. He clutched the table's edge to steady himself.

'Where is Pharaoh Seti?' a Nubian servant whispered in his ear. 'The ambassadors want to present him with the painted image of their princess.'

'He must have gotten one of his migraines,' said the scribe. 'Please make his apologies to our guests. I'll go have a word with him myself.'

§

'How could you be so stupid?' Amenhotep wailed. Seti sat grinning at his own reflection in the pharaoh's mirror of polished bronze. Tenderly he dabbed away the cosmetics he'd used to accent his almond eyes:

'So what's stupid about making a point that you and the others can't accept? I told you before I'm sick and tired of trying to govern this country.'

'There is no day devoid of its duties, my lord. It is your duty to govern Egypt'

'My heart isn't in it anymore. I'd rather be a dancing girl. You can't imagine the thrill of it, Amy, like a fire singing inside of me: all those men adoring me, and lusting after me in their hearts.' Jumping up Seti whirled around the room again, snapping his fingers in time while the fat scribe looked on in dismay. He pinched Amenhotep's bulging rump: 'You can't understand me. You're a eunuch.'

Clutching his clean-shaven head, the scribe closed his eyes and muttered a prayer to Isis.

'You're in a pious mood this evening,' Seti teased.

'My lord, the gong of fate has sounded. The evil High Priest is conspiring against us.'

'Herihor? That old stick? I should have him drowned in the Nile.'

'Some of your servants must know of your escapade tonight.'

Examining his own, long fingernails, Seti didn't answer.

'My lord, this can only add fuel to Herihor's claim that you're unfit to rule. I wouldn't be surprised if he's writing to the Hyksos kings, seeking their help to overthrow you. We must move at once to thwart him.'

'And what do you suggest?' Seti tried to look serious.

'I've told you about the scarab of Thutmose. After years of searching I've learned where it is.'

'No kidding, Amy. Where?'

'The Great Pharaoh tried to take it with him.'

§

'You think this is a good idea?' Seti whimpered, and Amenhotep nodded. Inside Thutmose's burial chamber, lit by the torches they'd brought to his tomb cut deep into the Valley of the Kings, four brawny servants wrestled with the Great Pharaoh's inner casket.

It had taken them hours to pry the lid off his stone sarcophagus, and raise the outermost casket of gilded wood, which held the middle one. Nestled in this lay his inner casket, of solid gold.

'What if some awful curse falls on us for violating his tomb?' Nervously Seti smoothed the Bedouin headdress he'd donned as a disguise.

'We have to take that risk,' said the scribe.

Amenhotep had organized their midnight voyage down the Nile and camel caravan to the tomb. He'd bribed its night watchmen with his own golden collar. Now he set a fresh torch into the holder that he, with his usual foresight, had brought along:

'I doubt the Great Pharaoh will mind if we borrow his amulet once. He was a good and wise ruler, who only wanted the best for Egypt.

'Don't worry, men,' he addressed the servants he'd handpicked for this delicate work. 'Once we've accomplished our sacred rite, we'll put everything back just as was. We won't steal a hair from Thutmose's head, or a dried pea from his burial goods. Now please let us see the great king himself.'

The servants bent and lifted the stiff old mummy, with its golden mask, out of the inner case. Shuddering they laid Thutmose gently on the pavement of his tomb.

'Please leave us now,' Amenhotep soothed. 'Wait for us in the shaft.' With looks of relief the men hurried out, stepping around the chariots, models of sailing ships and stacks of food containers the Great Pharaoh needed in his afterlife.

His plump fingers trembling, Amenhotep pulled off the mask of solid gold that covered Thutmose's head, neck and upper chest. Like the rest of the mummy these were swathed in stiff, dark bandages centuries old:

'He's probably wearing 100 amulets, all wound up with his packing.'

Seti touched the mummy's shoulder. 'Ooh, he's all sticky.'

'Don't touch him, my lord. He's preserved with tree resin.'

'Amy, I'm afraid!' As if blown by a spirit, the lone torch flickered on its stand.

'Don't worry, my dear.' The scribe drew a short, sharp knife from inside his kilt, the kind he used to trim papyrus to make proper scrolls. 'The scarab we're after should be over his heart—or where his heart was, before the embalmers cut it out to preserve in a canopic jar. I just have to probe these bandages. Please let me concentrate.' He bent over the mummy.

'Oh don't hurt Thutmose!'

'He's safe with Osiris in the Realm of the Dead. Nothing we do can hurt him. Wisest of Pharaohs,' the scribe wheedled, 'Lord of the Two Lands, Eye of Ra, please don't begrudge your servants the use of your magic scarab, just this once. It's an emergency.' He fumbled with the sticky bandages. 'I feel something hard.'

He drew out a piece of lapis-lazuli the size of his palm, dark blue like the evening sky and carved in the shape of a sacred dung beetle. 'Praise be to Isis, here it is. Thank you, oh wise Thutmose.'

'Let me see.' Seti snatched it.

'Wait, my lord, I need to prepare our rite.'

Seti held the scarab near the blazing torch. 'These hieroglyphs say nothing about wisdom. They say, 'I shall give you what you lack.''

'Do put that down. We're not ready.'

Seti's eyes opened wide, and he moaned.

'What is it?' cried the scribe.

'Too late,' he breathed. He touched his own slender chest, where two lovely maiden breasts had swelled.

'Oh dear Isis,' Amenhotep swore.

Patting himself between the legs, Seti laughed out loud. Raising his hands high over his head he stretched himself voluptuously, as if waking from a life of sleep.

'Thank you, dear Isis,' he sang out and his voice sounded sweet and high. 'For you have granted me *what I lacked*.' Falling on his knees he kissed the sticky mummy: 'Thank you Great Pharaoh, Eye of Ra—and thank you, my dear head scribe.'

Now Seti started to dance around the cluttered tomb. Faster and faster he whirled, while Amenhotep watched, sick at heart. Seti's headdress slipped off, revealing new yards of silky, black hair, which glittered in the torchlight like a waterfall reflecting all the stars of heaven.

§

The sun had climbed the desert's edge, tinting the low dunes pink and gold, when the two returned to their fishing boat moored in the Nile. A team of four spotted oxen was waiting to tow it upstream.

Amenhotep had swathed Seti in the servants' cloaks, to conceal his feminine form. Then he'd sent them back by caravan to the palace in the capital.

Now Seti asked nervously: 'Where are the sailors who crewed us downstream?'

'Ahoy there,' the fat scribe called. 'Shake a leg, sailors. We've no time to waste.'

'Indeed!' roared the High Priest of Amun-Ra, stepping from the striped sun tent on the deck with a pair of palace guards. Amenhotep nodded to the guards, whom he recognized.

'What's the meaning of this?' cried Seti, pitching his voice like a man's. 'I'm the Pharaoh of Upper and Lower Egypt. '

'High Priest, this is treason,' Amenhotep exclaimed. 'Lower your spears, my dear guards, or you'll answer to a military court.'

Grudgingly the armed men complied, eying the pharaoh curiously.

'Come, let us parley,' the scribe urged Herihor, pointing at the shady tent.

'Let us return to Thebes together,' the priest suggested with chill warmth.

'Fine, that will suit us,' said Amenhotep, and Seti cast him an anxious look.

§

Having settled himself on a pillow in the tent, across from the pharaoh and his scribe, pompously old Herihor began: 'My lord of the Two Lands, Eye of Ra, I apologize for barging in. Believe me, I am acting for your good.'

'And what do you know of my good?'

'In a moment, my lord, you shall see what I know. May I help you to unfasten your cloaks?'

'No thanks. I am feeling rather chilly.' Seti pulled his cloaks around him, despite the morning's furnace heat.

'Our pharaoh has a touch of fever, I'm afraid.' Amenhotep made smoothing motions upwards on his own bald head, and Seti tucked a lock of long black hair back underneath his Bedouin headdress.

'My lord,' said Herihor smugly. 'I think you should know that your head scribe is a *woman*.'

'That's absurd.' Seti guffawed. 'Eunuchs grow breasts, everybody knows.'

'And what about the other tools of a man?'

'Can a priest tell us of such tools?' the scribe countered.

'Amenhotep, we are private here. I demand that you drop your undergarment. Reveal to our pharaoh what you are.'

The scribe only folded his hands on his belly.

'If you are a eunuch—as I've always believed—why do you hesitate?' asked Seti sharply. Sweat dripping down his twitching face, for once Amenhotep seemed at a loss ...

Having pulled away from the bank, the boat slowly made its way upstream. They heard a whip crack over the oxen towing it. They heard the sailors bantering:

'I see a crocodile.'

'And I see three.'

'Nobody should drink beer this morning and tumble into the Nile.'

Then Herihor seized Amenhotep's kilt. The scribe slapped his claw-like hand away. Standing up Amenhotep pulled a pouch from inside his waistband.

'What are you doing?' Seti cried.

'The scarab: you found it after all!' Herihor made a grab for it, but Amenhotep dangled it just out of reach:

'Look at this precious treasure.' He lunged to the side, tore open the tent and flung the scarab into the Nile.

'No!' Herihor dived after it, not even kicking off his sandals.

'Priest overboard!' a sailor bellowed. From the river rose a howl of anguish. The muddy waters of the Nile churned white, and then blood-red …

Amenhotep hung over the side, 'Looks like the crocodiles got him … Great Thutmose, forgive us; we've lost your amulet; not being half as wise as yourself…'

'Is everything OK in there?' cried a guard.

'Yes, our pharaoh's fine,' reported the scribe. 'Herihor made a dreadful mistake, though. May the crocodile goddess comfort him.'

§

Seti and the scribe sat alone in the tent, eying each other uneasily as the boat glided slowly back up the river, back towards the capital and its duties.

'So what's your story?' Seti demanded.

Amenhotep chuckled sheepishly. 'I am in fact a woman, a matter a million times true. But please don't tell a soul, my dear. I've lived so many years as a man I couldn't go back, not even in the afterlife.'

'You have deceived me all these years I relied on you. What a farce! And now I should pretend to be a man? Amy, you big fat hypocrite, I should feed you to the crocodiles.' Seti bounded to his feet and took a step, as if to call a guard.

'Wait. You wouldn't denounce *your own mother.*'

'*What?!*'

'I can prove it, Seti my lamb. Just look at my feet, these awkward feet—the wide gap between the big toe and the rest. Your feet are the same, but young and thin; like nobody else's feet in Egypt … Back when I was a trainee scribe, your dad and I had a passionate affair. I was slim and good-looking, and he liked boyish girls …'

Gaping, Seti plopped back onto a pillow: 'You passed as a man, to learn to write—in order to have a career?'

'Yes. And I was delighted to go on at the palace, and stay near you as you grew. Seti, I *like* being a scribe. I like counting beans and compiling archives. Your father always found me a practical help.'

'And what of my mother, who ran off to Nubia with a handsome general when I was five?'

'If she were your mother, could she leave you alone when your dear father died? Nefertutu was barren, so she agreed to raise you as her child. Come to me, Seti; let me embrace you, as I have yearned to all these years.'

Too exhausted by all these revelations to weep, they hugged each other for a speechless minute.

Seti broke away first. 'What are we going to do?' she demanded in despair. 'I'm a woman now, and you are too. How bizarre. Are the gods playing tricks?'

'My son—I mean, my dear daughter—I think we should go on exactly as before. We'll tell the court that you've gained weight. Too many honey cakes.' Amenhotep patted her own, ample belly. 'Or you've decided to become a eunuch. Then you wouldn't have to marry the Libyan.'

'No,' Seti declared with passion. 'I won't live a lie, like you. I'd rather leave the palace and live as a free woman. Let me dance for my bread and beer. Dancing's an honest trade in Egypt.'

Amenhotep wrung her hands. 'You do make a lovely dancer,' she said softly. 'But will you really leave me, now you've found me?'

'Call me Iset and I'll visit you, mother.'

'Oh let's not do anything until tomorrow ... I need time to think. How shall I break this strange news to the court? Maybe we should stage your own demise? Maybe I should write to the Hyksos kings and beg them to send us a male ruler?'

'I'll give you till the cock crows tomorrow,' said Iset, a sly look in her almond eyes. 'Then I'm out of here.'

§

Deep in the palace, in her small chamber, Amenhotep tossed and turned. Was Iset right? Was she a gross hypocrite? What under heaven should she do?

Having impersonated a scribe, if she revealed her sex to the court, her punishment would be certain death. She'd probably be skinned and boiled alive ...

Yet who was a scribe, if she was not? She was a scribe with all her heart. And what would Egypt do without her? The new dam almost done, new irrigation systems in the planning stage ... And what about her struggle to check the grasping priesthoods, always intent on enriching themselves at the expense of the poorest farmers?

She rose from her wooden cot: 'I'll toss a coin. Heads and I go on as I was, trying to assist our next pharaoh. Tails and I reveal my peculiar truth.'

As she groped in her purse for a coin, though, the chamber's door flung open. In barged a wide-eyed slave with a torch, and a band of armed guards and officials.

Had they discovered her secret? Would they spear her here and toss her into the Nile? She closed her eyes, pleading with Isis to protect her in the afterlife...

'Lord of the two lands, Eye of Ra.' A senior official held out a papyrus roll. 'Pharaoh Seti has left us to serve the goddess Hathor. He's appointed you successor to the throne. 'There's no better guide in Egypt,' he writes here, and we all agree.'

Amenhotep sat down hard on her rickety bed. The others waited for her word.

She took a deep breath and looked at them. 'Very well,' she said calmly. 'Now where's that report about the snails in the Nile that are hurting our fishing?'

Anna Sykora has been an attorney in New York and teacher of English in Germany, where she resides with her patient husband and three Norwegian Forest Cats. Writing is her joy, and to date she has placed 92 tales in the small press or on the web; most recently with *Nautilus Engine, Spectra, 10,000 Tons of Black Ink* and *The Loch Raven Review*. She has also placed 175 poems.

The Watchmaker of Filigree Street

by N. K. Pulley

Thaniel Steepleton was moving out of his flat. He didn't know where to yet, but it was something to do. Tomorrow was an important day at work, very important, and rather than worry today about the strong possibility of dying there, he preferred to worry about his tap water, which had lately produced several things that were still growing in a goldfish bowl. So at four o' clock on the grey afternoon of the twenty ninth of May in the year 1884, his half day off, he consulted the *The Times* for somewhere else to live.

He liked the noise that a newspaper made when you folded it. It was the only thing he liked about newspapers; he had to read them through spectacles, and spelling mistakes annoyed him because as a clerk he felt that bad spelling was one step away from bad speech, which was within hopping distance of being Welsh. Mr Penderly who lived upstairs thumped on the ceiling and dust trickled down into the crease in the paper. Thaniel turned to the back few pages for the advertisements. The bang came again and he hid under the table. He looked down the page.

MRS EVANS BOREDING HOUSE
For respectable gentlemen;
Must be quiet and like cat's.

'Christ,' he mumbled. He circled the advert anyway in case there was nothing else, but in the next column there was a Mr Holmes who needed to share the cost of his apartment in the unfashionable part of Kensington. That looked much more promising- Mr Holmes was familiar with grammar at least- and then at the very bottom of the crowded page there was a third note.

27 Filigree Street
House to share.
Must not hate children.
Ask for Mr Mori.

Thaniel wondered what kind of name Mori was; it sounded Italian to him, and he tapped his pencil against it uncertainly. He had been to Italy once and he wasn't sure he wanted to live with an Italian. They were all charming and good-looking and he doubted if his pride would be up to it, being as he was an ordinary Englishman of no great stature and no striking feature, apart perhaps from his serious eyes. The ceiling creaked and he bolted for the door.

Beyond this door was the grimy side of Westminster. All of London was fairly grimy from the combined smoke of the trains, the oil lamps, the steamers on the Thames and the factories, but the east of Westminster was grimy in a fascinating, complicated sort of way that Thaniel much preferred to the rolling countryside of Derbyshire where he had grown up. On the other hand, Derbyshire had fewer suspicious-looking people. Thaniel felt nervous as he went by some men who were leaning against the pedestal of Nelson's Column, smoking in a watchful way. They were talking to each other with Irish accents, he noticed. He gave them a wide berth. It was racism but the healthy kind, he happened to know. He had often wished this year that he had not been the one to receive the telegram from Scotland Yard: for six months now that telegram had plagued him with the urge to be elsewhere whenever he heard an Irish accent. He tried to put it out of his mind.

In the following hour he learned that Mr Holmes did chemistry experiments with exploding gherkins and that Mrs Evans ran more of a cattery than a boarding house. Shell-shocked and puffy-eyed, he trailed on to Filigree Street, which was the furthest away in Knightsbridge, and knocked on the door of number twenty seven. It was an old house with a birch tree in its garden and a slate roof that framed an arched window. He didn't let himself like it. There would be an Italian inside.

Slightly before he knocked, the door opened inward and haloed with empty space a delicate man who was not Italian. Instead he had slanted eyes and black roots in his light hair. Thaniel paused, wondering how somebody who needed to share a house could afford an oriental servant.

'Um, I'm looking for Mr Mori. There was an advert in the newspaper,' he explained.

'Yes, come in,' the man said in an English accent. Thaniel blinked and followed him through a passageway and into the warm parlour. It was bare except for a sunbeam and a piano. The foreigner gave him one of the cups of tea that were steaming on the edge of the hearth.

'Is he in?' Thaniel ventured.

'I'm Keita Mori.'

'I- oh,' said Thaniel, flustered. 'I'm sorry, I thought- well. I'm Thaniel. Thaniel Steepleton.'

Mr Mori sat down on the hearth to cross his legs and rest his forearm over his knee. He seemed to be waiting for something.

Thaniel hesitated. 'You said in your advertisement that I wasn't to mind children?'

Mr Mori held up one thin finger. 'Wait for it.'

'For ... what?' Thaniel said, beginning to feel unsettled in the silent house and the sparkling dust.

Through the wall there came such a shouting that Thaniel would have been unsurprised to discover a murder on the other side, but then it dissolved into the hysterical laughter of a herd of small children.

'No, that's fine,' he gushed, relieved.

'I hoped so. Would you like to see upstairs?'

'If you wouldn't mind,' said Thaniel, and was pleased to find a very clean, spacious room with no Mr Penderly and nothing crustaceous in the water from the new tap. 'Can I ask what you do for a living?' he said as they went back down the steep stairs.

'I'm a watchmaker.' Mori gestured to the open door opposite, where there was a workshop full of clockwork devices that were not watches, but Thaniel was distracted by the man's wrist. It could have belonged to a child, probably one with consumption. 'I came from Japan,' he added, wrongly but usefully interpreting Thaniel's stare. 'There's a war there and I find that London is as good a place to sell watches as Kyoto.'

'Is it very different?'

'No, of course it isn't. People have their families and their factories and their preoccupation with tea.'

Thaniel laughed. Mr Mori smiled too and Thaniel wished he would do it more often. The smile drew faint lines around his eyes like the cracks which appear beneath the varnish of old porcelain. It gave him the look of an expensive doll, made with great care but then abandoned in sunlight for many years longer than its childlike features intimated.

'May I sign the lease? The sooner I can move in the better, really. Is the day after tomorrow all right?' Thaniel asked.

'It's in the workshop,' said Mr Mori.

Thaniel followed. He knew that it was selfish to mislead Mr Mori, who must have thought his new tenant was unlikely to explode before paying the month's rent, but suddenly it was important to have something to look forward to in case he didn't explode. And he could look forward to living here. It was lovely, and besides, Mr Mori was too tiny to make half as much noise as Mr Penderly, even if he came downstairs every morning on a pogo stick.

Something of a vaguely biomechanical nature waved at them as they came into the workshop, while across the shelves and the worktop, thousands of workings clicked and sussurated.

Thaniel watched, fascinated, while Mori tried to prise the lease papers away from what seemed to be a small but determined clockwork spider. It let go with a huff of hydraulics.

Mori took no notice and instead looked down at Thaniel's pocket as he handed over the papers. 'Your watch is broken,' he concluded, once Thaniel had signed.

'How on earth did you know that?'

'It's a knack.' Without looking backward, he put his thin hand behind him and picked up one of the five or six watches sitting on the worktop. 'If you leave it with me you can have this one while I mend yours.'

'Oh. Thank you very much.'

Thaniel took the watch Mr Mori gave to him. When he opened it he found a watch-paper inside, a little circle of paper cut to fit precisely within the lid. There were patterns on it that must have been drawn under the microscope with pen nibs as fine as a strand of hair, and a complex etching of vines around Mori's name in copperplate script. He looked up and saw that Mori was watching him.

'I'll bring my things here on Friday after work. What do I owe you for the watch?'

'Nothing.' He looked up at him for a moment. He had very black eyes, Thaniel thought. It wasn't often you saw somebody with black eyes rather than brown, black that stayed black even in bright light. He could see small reflections of himself in them. With no change in his expression, Mr Mori seemed to lose interest and Thaniel knew that the strange man had decided the conversation was finished before he said anything. 'Take the umbrella, you can bring it back tomorrow.'

'Day after,' Thaniel reminded him. 'It will be a busy day tomorrow, I don't think I shall be away from Whitehall before nine.' He tried to say it firmly, as though leaving were certain, but he didn't think he succeeded. He looked at Mori and wished he would smile again. It would help to make the conversation seem inconsequential if he would smile, or at least not look so solemn with his mirror eyes.

'Well, I shall be here whenever you like.'

'It doesn't look cloudy,' Thaniel observed as he opened the front door.

'No, it's for tomorrow, there's going to be a storm.'

'But it's nearly June.'

Mori shrugged: he was only the messenger. Thaniel didn't ask him how he knew that he, Thaniel, had no umbrella of his own. He had an feeling, a prickling on the back of his neck, that said the man would be able to tell him the number and timetable of the train to Derby he'd left his own umbrella on. Of course it was a silly feeling and he was embarrassed about it, so he rounded things off quickly and said,

'I'll see you on the thirty first.'

'You're going to be all right tomorrow, Mr Steepleton.'

Thaniel froze. 'What?'

'You look very worried. There's no need.'

'Oh …' said Thaniel, who had signed the Secrets Act. He tried to think of an excuse that didn't have to do with Irish terrorists, but the reason he worked sending and receiving telegrams was that the more interesting professions of authorship and journalism were closed to him, on account of his having the imagination of a cashew nut. 'I'm not worried, it's just my face.'

Mori smiled. He stood in the doorway to see Thaniel go, slouching with one shoulder against the frame and his arms crossed as though somebody had cut all his strings. Thaniel hesitated at the garden gate to look at him but then gave himself a shake and took a cab home to try and get some sleep before an early start tomorrow, and what promised to be an exhausting day.

§

Thaniel worked at the Home Office as a telegraph operator. This week, communications traffic centred around an Irish group with a political agenda that relied heavily on high explosives. Thaniel hated them. Firstly, he had to spell all their consonantally overburdened words in Morse code, and after a week of it he felt sure that if the Gaelic spelling system were to be abandoned, a great deal of the hostilities in Ireland would cease: everybody would be much less annoyed once they stopped trying to say Siobhan.

Secondly was the threat that promised bombs in all public buildings today. The original had been delivered last year to a policeman, who had sent it on by wire to this office. To Thaniel's telegraph.

The senior clerk arrived just after Thaniel did. He climbed onto a chair in the middle of the office. It was just after midnight, two minutes into the thirtieth, but the entire communications staff of Whitehall was here, perhaps fifty men, setting up their telegraphs for what would probably be a twenty-four hour shift.

'Everyone!'

Everyone looked up and Thaniel paused halfway through winding a new reel of transcript paper into his machine.

'You're all aware of the threat sent to Superintendent Williamson of Great Scotland Yard by the Irish organisation Clan na Gael, and what it forecasts for today.'

The senior clerk looked around the silent room for a second. Everyone else followed his gaze, which seemed to catch on the far corner, where three policemen were standing. 'There is therefore a police presence in the Home Office today. They will be searching for explosive devices.'

Thaniel pressed his fingernails into the edge of his desk. He noticed his friend Fred wasn't here and couldn't help wishing that he'd been so sensible too. It had seemed patriotic when he'd agreed to work today. He had a horrible feeling he'd hoped to prove to himself that under his clerkly disguise he was a man of steel, which was unfortunate, because he was pretty sure now that he was really a man of cauliflower and cheese.

'Happily,' the senior clerk continued, 'there is no time for you to be afraid. You must work as calmly and moreover quickly as you can, for the bulk of communications coming through this office is enormous today. The branches of government must be able to speak to each other. Get to work.'

Thaniel finished setting the new transcript reel with fingers that shook a little. Once it was ready he tapped out the pile of messages on his desk until his hands ached. When they really began to hurt and his initial surge of adrenalin drained, leaving him aware that he was tired and thirsty, he paused to make himself some tea in the little staff room and took it back to his desk to drink. It was early morning now and the dawn was grey through the tall windows; so far no buildings had exploded, and the policemen, having conducted a full search of the Home Office, assured them that there were no bombs here. Thaniel wasn't so sure, but he was less terrified than before. In the hope of settling his mind he took out Mr Mori's beautiful watch to study more closely.

He liked clockwork in the same way he liked the complicated London streets, and hoping to have a better look at it, he clicked open the watch's back panel. Then he dropped it when it whirred and puffed up a little cloud of smoke that smelled of gunpowder.

'No- no, you can't do that, I was only looking-'

He jumped when an explosion came from Horse Guards just opposite. The telegraphers nearest the window dived under their desks. They all looked across the street, expecting to see the wreckage of a bomb, but found the training yard full of cavalrymen in unfortunate hats rehearsing for a parade.

'Are you talking to your watch?' said the young man across the desk in the ensuing ripple of slightly hysterical giggling.

'I'm having a falling out with Our Saviour,' Thaniel mumbled.

'Oh. Right.' The young man went back to his work and so did Thaniel, though he paused again when the watch broke into a joyful rendition of the William Tell Overture. He gave it a shake, a little hopelessly.

'Guess who.' Cold hands pressed themselves over his eyes. 'That's right. It's your excellent friend Frederick Pike, who has won his bet at the races and delivers to you your not insubstantial share.'

'Fred! Where have you been, today's the thirtieth-'

'Oh, the Irish are in the stone age, they're not going to blow anything up, don't be absurd-'

'I really don't think-'

'It's five pounds.'

Thaniel forgot about Clan na Gael. 'Get away!'

'Twenty to one,' said a happy Fred. 'Any luck finding somewhere to live? You went off yesterday to look, didn't you?'

'Yes, although I'm in two minds about the landlord, he's...' Thaniel paused and frowned at the watch, which had stopped singing. 'He's foreign.'

'Good, no unnecessary small talk if the chap can't speak English. What have you got an umbrella for? Blue sky outside.'

'I ... think it might rain,' said Thaniel, and when thunder cracked across London a few hours later, Fred gave him a considering look.

'I think I might invite you to choose my bets more often, dear boy. Lucky guess, eh? Don't suppose I can share that brolly on the way out?'

At quarter to nine, hands aching, they left together and began the walk up to Trafalgar Square, where the night cabs lurked in the rain. It was with a sense of cautious elation. Nothing had blown up; there was news from the Home Secretary himself that all possible lines of investigation had been completed, the Irish prevented, and so now there was an exodus of clerks trooping over cobbles that shone yellow with the reflections of the lamps. Thaniel felt like he was coming out for the first time after a long illness. He hadn't looked at lights or cobbles for months, and now they were bright and wonderful.

As they came up toward Great Scotland Yard, a small side street on the right that contained the police headquarters, Fred rose onto the balls of his feet and waved to a cabby who was coming from that way.

'Hoy! Farringly!'

'You're friends with everyone,' Thaniel murmured. Of course it was useful to be owed a favour by a cabman, but in general he found sociable people suspicious; he couldn't help feeling that they were angling for extra birthday presents.

In his pocket, Mr Mori's watch clicked through quickening gears, then screamed. It was a horrible, keening siren noise, incredibly loud for such a tiny thing. Thaniel stopped on the corner where Great Scotland Yard met Whitehall Street and looked around. The watch had been predicting things all day and now he half expected to be run over by a fire engine.

'Shut that thing up!' Fred bellowed.

'Oh! Right.'

He pulled it out to find a way to switch it off, but it wouldn't, even when Fred hit it with the knob of his cane. And then unprovoked it stopped.

Fred sighed. 'That really is the damnedest-'

A titanic bang made the ground leap. Glass and fire roared from the mouth of the Yard's street. Thaniel felt the wave of heat and saw Fred's friend Farringly fly across the road and smack into the iron railings outside the Home Office buildings. It all seemed to happen rather slowly; he saw a spray of typewriter keys drift by, and when he blinked his skin felt stiff from its coating of ash. Then all the noise was gone and there was a long spell of silence, filled with the shapes of the smoke and floating bits of paper.

'I meant blessed,' Fred gasped. His voice sounded distant and tinny. 'That really is the most blessed thing.'

Thaniel closed his fingers hard around the watch. Ten paces further and they would have been broken heaps next to Farringly.

'Um—we'd better help—'

'Yes—'

They hurried out into the rubble, which was hissing in the rain, but then policemen began arriving and pushed them back. Fred caught Thaniel's hand and pulled him across toward Trafalgar Square and the lines of puzzled cabbies standing by their horses, straining to see what was going on.

'What happened?' the nearest asked as he opened the cab door for them.

'Explosion,' said Thaniel, whose ears were making a high-pitched humming noise that he couldn't seem to shift.

'What, an accident?'

'Clan na Gael,' said Thaniel, pressing his hands against his ears, but it made no difference.

'What?'

'What?'

'What did you say?' Fred said loudly.

'The Irish!'

'Oh,' said the cabby, unsurprised.

The cab moved off through the misty rain. Thaniel stared out of the window, rubbing his thumb again and again over the face of the watch that had saved his life. The route to Fred's apartment took them past a smart clockwork shop whose lamps were still on, and with a mangled explanation about having the watch looked at, he stopped the driver and hurried out into the rain.

The shop was called Spindle's. Mr Spindle himself was inside, sitting at the desk in his shirtsleeves while he polished the back plate of a new watch. Everything was tidy and he was plainly finished for the day.

'Hello,' he said to Thaniel over his spectacles. 'Horrible weather, isn't it?'

'Yes. Um, I …'

Mr Spindle frowned. 'My dear man, you don't look well- good God, you're trembling, whatever is the matter?'

'I—there was—'

'Sit down,' he said, motioning to the stool opposite with his tiny screwdriver. Thaniel bumped onto it. His ears were still making squeaking noises. 'I'll fetch you some brandy-'

'I'm quite well, sir, please, if you could just tell me about this watch,' Thaniel croaked. He pushed the watch over the desk and then pressed his fingertips against his eyes, fighting hard to keep from bursting into tears. He had tried not to think about how the watch could have known when the bomb was about to go off, but thinking had happened in spite of him. If Mr Mori had known the exact time that the bomb was due to explode, his thoughts said, it would have been no great trouble to put an alarm on the watch. And if Mr Mori had known what time the bomb would go off, the only possible conclusion was that he was the one who had made it. The watch was some kind of warning, should he find himself by accident near Scotland Yard at the wrong time. He must, Thaniel realized, have given it away by mistake. There had been at least five watches on the worktop yesterday.

'I think you need a doctor-'

'Please! It's important!'

'Yes, of course,' murmured Mr Spindle in a soothing voice. He watched Thaniel for a moment longer to make sure there wouldn't be any more outbursts. Then, with long, spidery fingers, he lifted the watch by its chain and clicked the back open. Eight glass panels fanned out with a mechanical sigh.

'Ah,' said Mr Spindle. 'This is Keita Mori's.'

'How do you know?'

Mr Spindle glanced up. 'He's very whimsical. He makes clocks that run for weeks rather than hours, and self-correcting timers, I've never worked out how he manages that, and weather gauges and star dials. He made one that flew, once. There's no other clockwork-maker in London who would spend so much time on unnecessary extras.' He looked at the watch through his magnifying glass, which had a pearl handle. 'Hm. This is interesting, even for him. Come back here for a moment, I'll need to see it through a microscope.'

Thaniel didn't move. He kept expecting the floor to leap up like it had done near Scotland Yard, and the ringing noise was persisting.

'I don't need to know the interesting things about it,' he said. 'Just whether it has an alarm set to go off at sixteen minutes past nine tonight.'

Nevertheless Mr Spindle sat down on a high wooden chair and leaned down to his microscope. He twisted the brass knobs until one of the lenses was so near to the watch that it nearly touched the glass. 'My God.'

'It does,' Thaniel concluded.

'And any number of other things. Come and look-'

'I don't care. The timer, is it set for sixteen minutes past?'

'Yes. Why does that matter?'

Thaniel swallowed. 'It went off right before a bomb.'

Mr Spindle frowned slightly. 'May I ask if it has done anything else … predictive?'

'What? Why?'

Mr Spindle looked uncomfortable. 'Come and look.'

Thaniel came to stand beside him and put his eye to the microscope. It was focused on one of the glass panels. The clockwork that had seemed tiny when he had looked at it before was huge now, and behind it were much smaller, translucent parts that glittered and shone as they interlocked. 'What are those tiny ones?'

'I believe,' said Mr Spindle, 'that those are diamond cogs. Much smaller than a sixteenth of an inch and metal stops being workable, you need something much harder. It's probably worth a fair bit.'

Thaniel looked down at the watch, more sure than ever now that Mori had given him the wrong watch. Nobody gave away diamonds to a stranger on purpose.

Mr Spindle was too fascinated to notice Thaniel's silence. 'These panels all interlock when they lie flush, I can see that much, so they must work together. This piece here, that's a spirit gauge and there's a compass, do you see that? It isn't labelled, but it spins as I turn it.'

'Yes …'

'Yes, and the clockwork is connected to that, so your own motion must affect the workings somehow, although the parameters are set so infinitesimally I should be surprised if they were at all useful. This machinery would know if you twitched.'

Thaniel wasn't listening. He was too busy wondering what Mori was doing with diamonds. He was a clockwork maker who lived in a house he had to share, for goodness' sake. Payment for something then. The bomb, of course, but one bomb didn't cost a little fortune in diamonds.

Mr Spindle smiled. 'Is this one of his clever jokes?'

'Why?' Thaniel said, startled out of his wonderings.

'Well, from what you describe and what I've seen, Mr Mori has given you a watch that, by measuring the movements you make throughout the day against what I presume is clockwork that describes every motion you *could* make throughout the day, alters it workings accordingly and can therefore tell the time a few seconds ahead. You seem to have a watch that tells the future. Brilliant. He set you up to do this, didn't he?'

'I … what?'

'Excellent! Well, tell him he had me fooled for at least five minutes. It's a game we clockwork men play, you see,' he added cheerfully.

'Or a fiercely clever way to hide illegal diamonds,' Thaniel whispered.

'What?'

'I've got to go. There's more.'

'More what?' cried Mr Spindle as Thaniel bolted for the door.

'More bombs!'

§

Thaniel caught the next cab back to Filigree Street and fell out onto the pavement the instant it stopped. He had just reached the garden gate, slick with the rain, when Mori opened the door.

'Is everything all right, Mr Steepleton?' He sounded much less calm than he had done yesterday and his dyed hair was soft and untidy where he had pushed his hands through it too often.

'Where are the other bombs?' Thaniel demanded.

'What?'

'I can see what you've done. You've hidden your payment where nobody will ever look, and even if they do look, the watch is complicated enough to seem like it really could tell the future. No problem for you, you're a genius. As soon as you realized you'd given it to me by mistake, you tried to get it back, but Whitehall was locked down today and non-staff members wouldn't have been allowed in.' Thaniel was thinking as he spoke, his thoughts working far faster than they ever usually had call to, but he could feel it all clicking into place, one puzzle after another.

'All your watches do strange things, so you decided you'd play on that instead,' he continued. 'You paid Fred and the sergeant at Horse Guards to get their timing right and lo, the watch has correctly predicted things even before the bomb. Lesser frauds with newspaper cut-outs and clumsy photographs have gone just as far, so God knows what people would make of a forgery like this.' He had to pause for breath. 'But I won't tell anyone if you tell me where the other bombs are.'

Mori put his hand on the back of his neck as if it hurt. 'Mr Steepleton, if I were to have made any bombs, why would I have set up so elaborate a fraud as this when I could simply have given you an ordinary watch and avoided your suspicion at all?'

'Because you picked up the wrong watch! You made a mistake, people like you always do!'

Mori tilted his head and regarded Thaniel in the way of somebody who has been idly looking at a simple mathematical problem and has just decided to point his full faculties at it, having lost patience with his own slowness.

Thaniel felt angry with his calmness. 'Well? Aren't you going to-'

'-say anything, before you call the police?'

'Oh, yes, very—'

'—clever, you can tell what I'm going to say next, just like any cheap hack at the fair.'

Thaniel frowned at him. 'Pink—'

'—rhinoceroses. Elephants. Fairy armdillos. What's a pink fairy armadillo?' he added.

'Twas—'

'—brillig, and the slithy toves did gyre and gimble in the … wave, it's wabe actually, and you did that just to make me say it, didn't you?' Mori said, a touch crossly.

Thaniel stared for a long time. The ringing in his ears was gone at last and he could hear the rain. He broke down into the same hysterical giggling that had possessed some of his colleagues after the gunshots from Horse Guards this morning.

'I believe you,' he laughed. 'I believe you, which is wonderful really, because I shouldn't like to live with somebody who almost blew me to smithereens, I think it would be counted foolish by most right thinking …'

Mori put his arms around him just as the giggling dissolved into tears. Thaniel clung to him because there was nobody else.

'Come inside,' Mori said softly. 'I've made some tea.'

'Why did you give me the watch?' Thaniel whispered.

'To keep you alive. Now come in from the rain.'

'You said it would rain,' Thaniel mumbled.

'Yes. May I have my umbrella back?'

Thaniel gave it to him and was quiet while he watched him pour out the tea in the kitchen. At last he said, 'Why would you bother to keep me safe? We only met yesterday, I don't know you at all.'

Mori glanced up at him through the steam. To Thaniel's shock, he looked sad. 'No, I know you don't.'

Thaniel sat in silence for a moment. He wanted to say something comforting, perhaps even close his hand over Mori's small one where it rested now on the table between them, but he wasn't a tactile person and he couldn't think of anything to say to this stranger whose way of thinking and feeling he didn't know yet. He changed the subject instead. 'You know I always thought it didn't make sense, for Clan na Gael to announce their own plans months in advance. It was you who gave Inspector Williamson the message, wasn't it?'

'He gets his clocks fixed here,' Mori murmured.

'So where are the diamonds in the watch from?'

'An old engagement ring I bought at the pawn shop. They're not good quality.'

'My theory was much neater,' Thaniel said, play irritably. He took a sip of his tea, feeling much better. 'You didn't like to save Scotland Yard, then.'

'It was the ugliest building in London.'

'Remind me never to offend your sense of aesthetics.'

Mori frowned at him. 'A sense of aesthetics is important. Otherwise you end up in the Swiss Guard.'

'I suppose Clan na Gael's ringleaders will all be arrested now,' Thaniel reflected. 'It'll put a stop to the Irish much more effectively than if the bomb hadn't gone off.' He glanced at Mori and suspected that he had already thought of it, months ago.

'Working in stripy tights for a man in a dress,' Mori grumbled.

Thaniel grinned. 'They're an elite fighting force.'

'Probably because somebody behind enemy lines is offering a pair of proper trousers to the first one to finish.'

Thaniel decided that he had an over-developed sense of propriety and leaned across to close his hand over Mori's. 'Thank you for saving me,' he said.

'Hm,' shrugged Mori, but Thaniel saw the porcelain lines form around his eyes.

N. K. Pulley has just graduated after spending three years wandering around Oxford with a bewildered expression. After that she went to teach for a month or so in China, where people sometimes crossed the street to take a photo of her; this caused her to be even more bewildered, so now she mainly lives behind a laptop, looking up bits of Victorian history and learning Japanese. She likes London enough to write about it and she hopes to live there one day, possibly with a cat. For the moment, she's got a guppy called Charles.

Book Review:

Historical Fiction Writing: a practical guide and tool-kit by Myfanwy Cook

Paperback: 452 pages
Publisher: ActiveSprite Press (1 Mar 2011)
ISBN-13: 978-0956765406

Reviewed by Alex Neville

There are a few 'how-to' books on Historical Fiction that tell the would-be historical novelist how to research their novel, how to organize all the information and typical historical fiction writing problems. But what if you are a new writer and really don't have a clue of how to approach the actual writing of your novel? Cook's new book can help, with practical exercises, not only in how limber up for the serious business of writing, but also to consider your market and choose your topic.

Early on Cook tries to define what Historical Fiction is. Hence her themes of 'Chronology' and 'Band.' Cook's Chronology starts with Prehistory, Ancient Egypt, through individual centuries AD, then it comes to Multi-period, Timeslip and Historical Fantasy and Alternative History. These last four could surely be genres. Then at the end of Chronology comes Children and Young Adults, which could also be classed as genre. Maybe those categories should be listed under Band, which does seem to equate with genre – it mentions Adventure, Romance and Crime. All this just goes to show that it is a minefield trying to categorize historical fiction.

All of the big questions in Historical Fiction writing are covered in separate chapters – such as setting, creating a sense of place, creating a sense of period through dialogue, and historical accuracy, but they are not discussed in depth. There tend to be heated debates within the historical fiction world about how to write authentic sounding dialogue, how much detail should be included and authenticity. However this book concentrates on the functional aspects of writing Historical Fiction, rather than these debatable issues.

There are sections on the usual writing processes, such as theme and viewpoint. Of course there is a section on research, but it is relatively small compared to the rest of the book. Many tasks throughout the book involve researching such things as historical characters or sites anyway.

Each chapter concludes with activities for would-be novelists. These consist of various tasks often including going out somewhere to ask people their opinions (friends, book-sellers, library staff) as well as short writing tasks designed to make the writer think about various historical aspects, such as identifying the difference between the past and the present.

If you are intending to write a Historical Mystery, you are in luck, as this book has a whole section devoted to the genre. Interspersed throughout the book are tips and quotes from historical novelists. If you are a member of the Historical Novel Society, you will recognize most – if not all – of the usual suspects. There is also a chapter devoted to Top Tips from historical novelists saying what they think are the most important points to remember. So there's plenty of input from a wide range successful historical novelists, writing in various sub-genres.

The last section is devoted to the tasks of beginning to write and finishing touches. The book includes a glossary of words, defining the meaning of alliteration, farce and so on. There is also a list of useful books and websites, including those mentioned in the text. However, there is no index, and nor do the Contents Pages list actual page numbers. So getting around, and finding particular information can be difficult. However the book is arranged into six sections, with chapters and sub headings. At over three hundred pages of text, some illustrations could have brightened the publication up, but that is a minor point.

Because of its coverage of writing as a whole, not just the aspects particular to historical fiction, it is well worth having a copy to dip into to provide encouragement and inspiration. It does what it says on the cover: it is a practical guide and tool-kit for Historical Fiction Writing.

Book Review:

Ruso and the River of Darkness by R. S. Downie, Called Caveat Emptor in the US

UK Edition:
Paperback: 464 pages
Publisher: Penguin (3 Mar 2011)
ISBN-13: 978-0141036946

US Edition:
Hardcover: 352 pages
Publisher: Bloomsbury USA (December 21, 2010)
ISBN-13: 978-1596916081

Reviewed by Alex Neville

This is the fourth book in Ruth Downie's *Ruso* Roman mystery series. In the first book Ruso was a Roman army medicus who got drawn into solving a crime. On the way, he managed to acquire a sullen British slave girl called Tilla.

By book four, Ruso is out of the army due in part to injury, but also because his contract has finished. However, he now has quite a reputation for solving crimes. Romance has blossomed and he has married Tilla. He is also now in possession of a goodly quantity of nice Samian crockery, but has no house to store it in and. He is volunteered by a friend to help the Procurator's office investigate the disappearance of a large sum of tax money. It was being brought to Londonium from the town of Verulamium. The men tasked with delivering the money have also gone missing. Soon Ruso is hot on the trail, which leads to peril not just for himself, but for Tilla as well.

When I read the first in the series, I was interested, though not enough to actively chase up the sequels. The book was well written, but there was the sneaking suspicion that it might be jumping on the fashionable Roman historical mystery bandwagon. But this is not true. By the fourth book in the series, the writing is stronger than the first, and the story more compelling. Time has lent richness to the series and the lead characters have become more vivid. The Ruso series is firmly anchored in the Roman provinces. The lead character comes from Gaul, and is somehow – perhaps because of British Tilla—now attached to Britannia.

Downie's depth of research is impressive, but she does not bury the reader under detail, or let it get in the way of telling the story. The tale grows out of something that could easily have happened in early 2nd century Roman Britain – the theft of taxes. This allows the reader to see the workings of the Procurator's office, which was very much the civil service wing of the Roman administration. The Assistant Procurator is a rather young, short-sighted chap, who has only got the job due to family connections. He is thrilled by any opportunity to get out of the office, but also very earnest about his project to survey the milestones in the province, as ordered by Emperor Hadrian.

There's plenty of wry humour, with the citizens of Verulamium happy to have their reputation of being the town that always pays its taxes on time – they want to be as Roman as the Romans. Through this Downie illustrates Tacitus' observation that the Britons were enslaved by the lures of Roman civilization (Agricola, Chapter 21). However, at heart, the council members are noisy and volatile, and at one point Ruso reckons that British could not be accused of being boring. There are some amusing north-south comments: Tilla is from the north of the province, so finds the southerners attitudes rather odd at times, and vice versa. This neatly taps into present day Britain, so that a British reader at least can smile at the joke.

Downie's characterisations are excellent, allowing the players to stand out in the mind's eye. There are quite a few people in the book, and there is a handy character-listing at the front of the book. The story is told in third person from two views – that of Ruso himself and of Tilla, who has a few secrets she feels she needs to hide from her husband. The differing viewpoints are very effective, particularly when a worried Ruso does not know the location of his wife, but the reader does.

Overall, there is much pleasing detail in this book. As with most historical fiction set in this era, not everything is known about the workings of the province. But Downie sure-footedly makes the whole story very plausible and constantly intriguing.

Alex Neville is an archaeologist turned librarian and reads lots of historical fiction.

Book Review:

Rome Burning by Sophia McDougall

Paperback: 608 pages
Publisher: Gollancz (14 April 2011)
ISBN-13: 978-0575096936

Reviewed by Jared Shurin

Sophia McDougall's *Romanitas* series is set in a world in which the Roman Empire never fell. The initial point of divergence takes place in 192 AD after the Emperor Commodus had bankrupted the Empire. Following his assassination, the rule of Rome fell to Publius Helvius Pertinax. Pertinax began a series of legal and economic reforms, but they never saw fruit. His extremely short (three month) reign was also ended by assassination – this time by disgruntled members of his own Praetorian Guard.

In Ms. McDougall's version of events, Pertinax foiled the attempt on his life and lived to see his reforms put in place and then continued by his son. The Empire was pulled back from the brink of collapse. The series, begun in 2004, is set contemporaneously. When *Romanitas* begins, the world is divided into three major powers: Roman, Sinoan (Chinese) and Nionian (Japanese). A few areas, such as parts of Africa, remain independent. Others, such as Terranova (the Americas) have been divided between the various empires.

In *Romanitas*, the technology is established as roughly behind our own. A form of long-distance communication has been invented, as well as huge works of civil engineering, but there's little evidence of either computers or electronics. Society is also stagnant. Slavery still forms the backbone of the Roman economy and the hierarchical class system is well solidified. Rome is, above all, still an Empire – ruled and limited by the vision of a single man.

Romanitas is a very focused story—a geographically limited footrace for personal survival on the part of its protagonists. As one of the main characters, Marcus, is heir to the empire, the stakes are still high, but, as a text, *Romanitas* is focused very much on the fate of three individuals.

Its sequel, *Rome Burning,* goes epic.

Rome Burning was first published in 2007 but has recently been released in a new, re-edited edition. Set three years after the events of the first book, Marcus is back in Rome and established as the Emperor-in-Waiting. Theoretically, life should be easier for our motley trio of heroes, and on the surface, it is. His companions, Sulien and Una, are now freed from slavery. Sulien is a doctor at a charity clinic for slaves, a quixotic effort that struggles along through Marcus' patronage and the moral blackmail of Rome's industrial leaders. Una serves Marcus' informal advisor and even more informal lover. Her uncanny ability to read minds makes her an invaluable assistant, and, no matter how politically awkward it may be, the two of them are very much in love.

Nothing's ever easy and our heroes are facing problems both old and new. Marcus' conniving cousin, for example, is still lurking around the fringes, feverishly plotting to take the throne for himself. Although no longer heir to the throne, Drusus is convinced that he *will* be Emperor.

Marcus is also finding that his proposed reforms, especially his desired end to slavery, simply aren't happening. The Empire is too bogged down in its economic and cultural quagmire to enact any change of that magnitude. Marcus and Una's old allies, an underground network of escaped slaves, have all but given up hope in Marcus. Their loss of faith stings our heroes deeply.

Everything rapidly comes to a head in *Rome Burning* when Marcus' uncle, the Emperor Faustus, falls ill. Faustus is still the indecisive, muddle-headed Claudian figure he was in *Romanitas*, but he at least serves as a buffer between the barely-adult Marcus and the burdens of state. When events conspire to make Marcus the regent, he's now dealing with Rome's problems as well as his own.

And Rome's problems are *much* larger than Marcus'—Rome *is* burning. Rome, the city, is attacked by terrorists, presumably agents of the rival Nionian empire. Rome, the empire, is also under siege. The Roman wall in Terranova, the great structure that splits the two empires, is proving porous. Nionian and Roman skirmishes are becoming more and more frequent with greater and greater consequences. As much as Marcus would rather spend his regency quietly pushing along his domestic agenda, his first order of business is to avert global war.

What follows is a much grander adventure than the preceding novel. Marcus, Una and Sulien, as well as their friends Lal and Varius, are scattered not just around Rome, but around Asia as well. The Sinoan and Nionian Empires, Rome's equally decadent and compelling global rivals, are both explored at length. Terranova also comes alive in more detail through despatches from the front and high-level conversations between the Emperor's advisors. There's a greater sense of drama as well—more bloodshed, more sneaking about, more explosions and more grand processions. This isn't a case of cinematic sequelitis, this is the rational result of Marcus' new position in life: if *Romanitas* was the tale of three relative insignificants, *Rome Burning* is the story of *the most important man in the world*.

Fortunately, some things don't change. Ms. McDougall continues to foil the detail-heavy traditions of genre by maintaining a tight frame on the characters. Their journeys take them into more exotic locations, but the reader still only sees them through the protagonists' eyes. In a recent interview with Ms. McDougall, she was asked about her authorial decision to keep the characters 'away from the action'. There are *battles* happening somewhere, but we only hear about them through the news. Ms. McDougall's answer was telling: the characters *are* where the action is. The conflict in *Rome Burning* isn't a war; it is about preventing the war. One of the key lessons of *Rome Burning* is that there's nothing majestic about violence. Marcus and Una, despite their youth, understand this. Their struggle to keep the world from war and terrorism comes as an extension of that belief; their opponents are those that would callously use destruction as a valid tool for political ambition or jingoistic fulfilment. The action *witnessed* in *Rome Burning* supports this philosophy. It is nasty, bloody and un-chivalric. It isn't about heroism; it is about death.

Ms. McDougall also continues the romantic tragedy that is Marcus and Una's relationship. *Romanitas* firmly established their star-crossed love. They're a good pair, but a mature one; they're fully aware of the yawning chasm between their social standings. At the start of *Rome Burning*, Una's elevated social status (that is, from 'slave' to 'free and awkward') has allowed them a discreet relationship, but they both still accept its impermanency. In *Rome Burning*, its end is nigh. Becoming betrothed is Marcus' diplomatic ace in the hole and Marcus is forced to spend it. Without going into the details about the unusual new character that Ms. McDougall introduces, it is simply worth mentioning that the author handles the situation with her usual tact. Ms. McDougall's ability to create human, empathetic, and ultimately soul-destroying scenarios is on full display here.

My sole frustration with *Rome Burning* is regarding the conclusion. It ends on a cliff-hanger—a large one. With *Savage City* out in May, readers will now never have to worry about resolving it. But, as a matter of taste, I prefer a book that, as China Miéville phrases it, 'begins, middles and ends'. Marcus and Una keep up a manic pace in *Rome Burning*. Given how seductively empathetic they are, by the book's conclusion, I think that both they and the reader deserve some intratextual respite.

Rome Burning is the best of both worlds. It maintains *Romanitas'* excellent tradition of elegantly scripted, character-focused SF but also increases the stakes with high-powered political tension, global conflict, operatic romance and dire treachery. *Rome Burning* is not a *better* book than *Romanitas*, but it is a more *evolved* one. With her debut out of the way, Ms. McDougall uses *Rome Burning* to confidently address greater problems with no less talent.

Jared Shurin's reviews and non-fiction have appeared in *The Hub*, *Weaponizer*, *The Literary Platform* and *Pornokitsch*. He's a native of Kansas City and currently lives in London. In this timeline, at least.

Made in the USA
Lexington, KY
01 July 2011